RESURRECTION

REDEMPTION HARBOR SERIES

Katie Reus

Cover art: Jaycee of Sweet 'N Spicy Designs
Editor: Julia Ganis
Author website: http://www.katiereus.com

Resurrection/Katie Reus. -- 1st ed.
KR Press, LLC

ISBN-10: 1635560152
ISBN-13: 9781635560152

eISBN: 9781635560145

For my incredible sister. Thank you for everything.

Praise for the novels of Katie Reus

"...a wild hot ride for readers. The story grabs you and doesn't let go."
—*New York Times* bestselling author, Cynthia Eden

"Has all the right ingredients: a hot couple, evil villains, and a killer action-filled plot. . . . [The] Moon Shifter series is what I call Grade-A entertainment!" —Joyfully Reviewed

"I could not put this book down. . . . Let me be clear that I am not saying that this was a good book *for* a paranormal genre; it was an excellent romance read, *period.*" —All About Romance

"Reus strikes just the right balance of steamy sexual tension and nail-biting action....This romantic thriller reliably hits every note that fans of the genre will expect." —*Publishers Weekly*

"Prepare yourself for the start of a great new series! . . . I'm excited about reading more about this great group of characters."
—Fresh Fiction

"Wow! This powerful, passionate hero sizzles with sheer deliciousness. I loved every sexy twist of this fun & exhilarating tale. Katie Reus delivers!" —Carolyn Crane, RITA award winning author

"A sexy, well-crafted paranormal romance that succeeds with smart characters and creative world building."—Kirkus Reviews

"*Mating Instinct's* romance is taut and passionate . . . Katie Reus's newest installment in her Moon Shifter series will leave readers breathless!"
—Stephanie Tyler, *New York Times* bestselling author

PROLOGUE

Colt Stuart looked through his government-issued binoculars at the terrorist bastard beating the shit out of one of his subordinates for whatever imagined slight. The guy working for their target was no saint either, but still. "What a pussy," he muttered.

"Hey!" Flat on her stomach, the sexy redhead perched on the hill with him gave him a dirty look before returning her gaze to the scope of her custom Remington 700.

Or he assumed it was a dirty look, because he didn't look directly at Skye Arévalo, his new partner of two weeks in the CIA. Because when he did, it was hard to focus and hard to hide his attraction to her. For a multitude of reasons. Everything about her called to him on the most primal level. "What?" he asked.

"You like pussy?"

Okay, *now* he looked at her. Was this a trick question? "Uh, yeah?"

She lifted an eyebrow, her ice blue eyes cold. "You respect pussy?"

"Hell, yeah." Didn't even have to think about that.

"Then don't insult it by calling him a pussy. Call him what he is. A dick. Or an asshole."

His lips kicked up as he drank in her pissed-off expression. "I'm pretty sure I'm going to marry you."

She stared at him with horror in those Mediterranean-blue eyes before rolling said eyes and turning away to look back through the scope. "You've got problems," she muttered.

7

"Is it inappropriate that I like it when you say the word pussy?" he murmured, returning to his binos and trying not to imagine what she'd look like naked. Trying and failing.

For this mission they'd had to change clothes in tight quarters and she'd had no issue stripping down to her boyshort panties and sports bra in front of him. She was average height, lean and ridiculously sexy. When he'd seen the text on the back of her panties—*Badass with a good ass*—he'd fallen just a little harder for her.

"Pretty sure that's sexual harassment, dude."

"File a report." They were working undercover, basically didn't exist to the civilian word. There would be no report to file.

She snorted at the ridiculousness of his words. "To answer your question, yes, it's inappropriate. But it's okay. I like inappropriate."

He wasn't sure how to respond to that. Wasn't sure how to respond to most things that came out of Skye's mouth—a woman who carried C4 in her purse and called it "being prepared," as if she was a freaking Boy Scout. The one thing he was sure of: he hadn't been kidding about that marriage comment. Not locking down this woman would be pure *insanity*. Because he was pretty damn sure there was no one else in the world like her. And even if he was *also* pretty damn sure she was a little crazy, he liked her brand of it.

"You've got a clean shot," he murmured. For this mission they'd literally done rock, paper, scissors to decide who was behind the rifle. Her idea, of course. He was pretty sure she'd cheated too.

"Yeah I do." She pulled the trigger

.

CHAPTER ONE

—Against all odds and logic, we hope.—

Fourteen months later

Colt banged his fist against the door, fear and the smallest bit of hope punching through him. "Answer the fucking door," he snarled. "Open, or I kick it in."

"Maybe you should take it down a notch." Next to him, Brooks shoved an agitated hand through his hair, his Stetson held loosely at his side.

"And maybe you should be freaking out more." One of their best friends had been holed up in his home for weeks, refusing to talk to anyone, to see anyone. Colt didn't know exactly what his friend was going through, but he'd lost a lot of damn friends in the sandbox and the only woman he'd ever loved had died too. Something he couldn't think about right now. He couldn't focus on his own pain when he could help his friend, when he had a damn purpose.

Mercer had recently lost his wife, and the man wasn't handling it. The guy had been in love with Mary Grace since he was fifteen. They'd been each other's world. And two months ago she'd been killed in Mexico, a victim of cartel violence. Allegedly.

Colt hadn't been in love with Skye since he was a kid, but eight months with her sure felt like a lifetime. Hell, when she died it felt like he'd lost part of himself. The only part that

9

mattered. He had to force himself out of bed every day, to shove back the emptiness. So on one level, he understood how Mercer felt. He shoved that thought right back inside where it belonged and ignored it. He couldn't fix his own problem, but he could help out Mercer.

Panic swelled through Colt as the seconds ticked by without any response from inside—until he heard cursing on the other side of the door. Good. If his friend was cursing, he was alive. A solid minute later the lock snicked loudly as it twisted open.

Colt grabbed the handle and shoved it open, pushing past his best friend in case he tried to slam the door closed in his face.

Mercer, wearing boxers and nothing else, had grown a full black beard and his dark eyes were glassy. "What the hell are you doing here this early?"

"First, it's two o'clock in the afternoon. Second..." Colt hauled off and punched him right in the nose. He needed to wake Mercer the hell up. Violence was pretty much the only way to do that now.

"Ah, hell," Brooks muttered as Mercer flew back and fell on his ass with a grunt.

He held a hand to his nose, looking more alert than he had in two months as he glared up at Colt and Brooks. "What the hell, man?" His voice was muffled as he tried to stop the bleeding.

"I believe this is called an intervention," Colt said, stepping into the foyer, cringing at the stench. "God, it smells like old pizza and cow crap in here. Mary Grace would kick your ass if she saw you living like this."

"Don't say her name!" Mercer shoved to his feet, letting his hand drop. Blood dripped down his face as he snarled at Colt. His teeth were toothpaste commercial white against his dark brown skin. Right now he looked like a rabid wolf baring his teeth at them.

"I'll say her name if I want." Yeah, he knew he was being harsh, but this was what Mercer needed. He needed to feel something, to wake the hell up. And making Mercer angry was the only way Colt knew how. Because the guy sure wasn't going to talk about his fucking feelings. He needed to get out of this rabbit hole he'd let himself fall into. "We all lost her. Every single one of us."

Most days Colt couldn't believe she was gone. They'd all grown up together, and in his case, he'd been friends with Mary Grace since they were five years old. She was like a sister to Colt. Hell, he was still holding on to the hope that she wasn't actually gone. It was why he was about to get on a plane in two hours and see if the tip he'd received was right. But first he had to make sure one of his best friends didn't do something stupid while he was gone.

"Mary Grace."

"Ah, hell," Brooks said again, clearly not going to intervene. Just muttering his standard curse.

"Fuck you," Mercer snapped, taking a step toward Colt.

That was it. *Get angry*, he silently willed his childhood friend. Mercer needed anger to replace the grief. God, or at least mute it. Just for a week. That was all Colt needed. Because if Mary Grace was alive, he was bringing her home to his best friend. He just couldn't give Mercer the hope she was alive. Because if he did and it turned out she wasn't... It would destroy him. "Mary. Grace."

Mercer rushed at him like a bull. But he was too slow. Colt smoothly sidestepped as Mercer flew past him.

Colt swiveled to face his friend, hands on his hips. "Couple months ago I'd have never even been able to punch you. Now you can't even tackle—"

Mercer sprung like a wildcat, tackling Colt like the linebacker he'd been in college. Colt's back slammed against the wood floor, jarring him to his bones. When Mercer punched him in the ribs, Colt twisted, slammed his elbow across the man's face and slid out of his hold. His friend had played pro ball so he wasn't worried he'd do much damage to Mercer. He needed more from the guy right now.

He'd barely put a foot of distance between them when Mercer lunged again, looking like a wild animal as he attacked.

"Stay back!" Colt shouted at Brooks when his friend made a move to step in, his boots thumping against the floor. Mercer needed to let out his aggression, needed to fight someone.

He took the blows Mercer rained down on him. Though he knew Mercer was holding back. Colt wouldn't be breathing otherwise. He was vaguely aware that they'd broken the banister at the bottom of the stairs and put at least two holes in the wall next to the living room entryway as they fought. Good. Fixing those things could be projects for Mercer. Anything to keep his hands busy while Colt was gone.

When Mercer's last blow barely grazed Colt's side, he pulled him into a tight grip, more an awkward hug than anything.

Mercer stilled and then put his arms around him in a harsh grip, his head on Colt's shoulder as his giant body trembled with silent tears. "I don't know how to live without her," he rasped out.

Colt's throat tightened. "I know." It was on the tip of his tongue to say he was going to get her back. But he couldn't give Mercer that kind of hope if it turned out to be false. He simply couldn't. "But you've got to. I've gotta go out of town for a week and Brooks is gonna stay here with you."

Mercer shoved back then. The scent of Jack Daniels wafted off him. "I don't need a babysitter."

Brooks stepped up to tower over them, his expression tight. "Good, because I'm not gonna be wiping your ass or cooking you dinner. And I'm not asking. I'm staying, so deal with it." Gone was the relaxed cowboy, replaced by the stone-cold sniper he'd once been.

Mercer watched them both for a long moment before shoving to his feet. "You two do whatever the hell you want. You always do," he muttered before turning to stalk down the darkened hallway.

Colt followed suit and stood as well. There were absolutely no lights on anywhere that he could see. Mercer's home was a tomb, the once bright and cheery home gone. "This place is disgusting," he said to Brooks. "Hire a company to clean it up. I'll pay for it. And make sure he eats while I'm gone. Just...keep him alive."

"I'm not gonna off myself!" Mercer shouted from somewhere in the house.

Colt wasn't so sure. Mercer seemed one drink away from going all "Whiskey Lullaby" on them. Brooks agreed, if his concerned expression was any indication.

Brooks tilted his head once toward the open front door. "I'll walk you out," he murmured. Once they were down the steps and headed to the driveway, he said, "You sure about this?"

"No." Because he wasn't sure about anything. The only thing he knew was that there was a chance Mary Grace was alive. And he was damn sure going to get her back if he could. Colt might not be able to do anything about the woman *he* loved being gone, but he could try to bring Mary Grace back to Mercer.

Brooks looked at the house. "We should tell him."

"No way. If my tip is wrong..." Colt shook his head, slid his sunglasses down over his eyes without finishing the thought. *It really* will *kill him.*

Brooks scrubbed a hand over his face, nodded. "If you need backup—"

"I'll call." Which he wouldn't. This was for him to do. He couldn't search for Mary Grace if he was worried about Mercer putting a bullet in his own damn head, so Brooks had to watch him. Plus Brooks had a softer touch than Colt.

"We should let the others know too."

Colt knew who he meant, but he shook his head. "No. They've all got busy lives."

"They'd drop *everything* for this."

True enough. Growing up, there had been seven of them who'd been inseparable. All best friends, including Mary Grace. A couple of the guys hadn't joined the crew until around eleven or twelve, but the seven of them, once they'd become friends, had become more like family. Everyone had come home to Redemption Harbor, South Carolina once she'd died. Gage, Leighton, Savage and Colt had all moved away but nothing could have kept them from coming home for that. Mercer had refused to have a funeral, said there was no point without a body. Because the truth was, the man couldn't let go.

"I know." But he also knew he was going to break a shit-load of laws in the next week. And he didn't much care. To the outside world, he worked for a security firm—in the accounting department. In reality, he was a spy for the CIA who got the job done when necessary. But even his boss wouldn't know what he was about to do. "It'll be easier for me to travel alone. I'll draw less attention this way. For the return trip, I might need your dad's plane if—"

"I've got the pilot on standby."

Thank God. "He might have to cross the border illegally."

Brooks gave him a wry smile. "I know."

Colt nodded once. There was nothing else to say. He was about to head into cartel territory in Mexico on a freaking tip. Luckily for him, the US government had spent a few million dollars training him to become invisible and invincible.

Time to put all those years and that money to good use.

* * *

Mary Grace tensed as Arturo Ramirez's bedroom door opened, but it was just his oldest son, David. Him, she could deal with. It was the youngest brother who was unstable.

Even though she wanted to punch the man in the face, she pasted on her neutral doctor smile as she stood from her recliner next to the bed where the aging, dying drug lord lay asleep. And as long as he was alive, she was too. "He's just dozed off."

"Is he in pain?" David asked, his expression one of real concern. The man truly loved his father—unlike his brother Rafael, who hated Arturo.

"Not right now, no." Even though she hated the family that had kidnapped her, and hated being here, she was still a doctor first. And Arturo was her patient for as long as he was alive. And she wanted to make sure he stayed that way because he was necessary for her survival. Which, unfortunately for her, wasn't going to be much longer. She needed to find a way to escape before Arturo died or she was dead for certain.

"Good." David turned to face her now, all civil politeness. The man had gone to Columbia Business School and was highly intelligent. Not only that, he was married with two kids and she'd seen him with his children once. He loved them dearly. She'd also seen him drive a blade straight into a man's skull without changing his expression. "Do you need anything? Are you hungry? I heard you skipped lunch."

"Ah, I'm okay." She'd skipped lunch because she had morning sickness. She hadn't let anyone here know she was pregnant yet. She was pushing three months and wouldn't be able to hide it much longer. Her belly had already popped but she was small and wore loose shirts. "I have a little stomach bug but I'll get some crackers later."

He looked at his father, then back at her. "Come now. You should eat some."

She didn't argue because she'd learned two months ago that it was useless. Not only that, it was stupid to disagree over small things. She needed everyone in this house to think she was weak, submissive and resigned to being a captive. The truth was, she would likely die here, but she had to keep hope alive. For herself, her unborn baby, and for a husband she missed more than anything in the world. She desperately wanted to get home to Mercer. A man she'd loved before he'd become a man, before she'd known what love even was. They'd been kids when they'd fallen for each other, and the thought of dying without seeing him again? She swallowed hard. She couldn't break down in front of this man.

"How is he doing? No lies." David's voice was low as they stepped out into a mosaic-tiled hallway.

The palatial estate was in the Mexican countryside on a huge horse ranch. She'd gleaned enough bits of information over the last couple months that she knew roughly where the nearest town was. Not that she was certain she'd go there anyway if she escaped. Not when the Ramirez family basically owned local law enforcement throughout this region of the country. Hell, she wouldn't go to any *policía* for help. If she escaped, she'd call her husband and friends back home for a way out of here. That was neither here nor there, however. She needed to stay focused on her conversation with David.

"He's doing as well as can be expected. Some moments he's lucid and others...he drifts in and out, but he's not in pain." She had him on enough pain meds to ensure that. There was no cure for stage four pancreatic cancer—that had spread to his other organs—but she could make him as comfortable as possible in his final days. He was still in a lot of pain though.

"Good. That's good." He nodded at one of the guards standing next to an open archway along the hallway. The man held an AK-47 with ease.

She'd gotten used to the sight of weapons. Everyone here had one—whether it was a machine gun, pistol, or a machete, everyone was armed. Even the onsite chef carried a gun. The guard gave her a small nod and polite smile. She recognized him as one of the men she'd helped patch up after he'd been thrown from a horse. He wouldn't hesitate to kill her if ordered, but hey, he was polite now, and he'd been grateful when she'd mended his wound. She'd take it.

"How much time do you think he has?"

Even though she didn't like David, she didn't think he was asking from a bad place. Which was weird to think. She wanted to paint this guy with broad strokes as a monster. Which he definitely was. And if she got the chance, she'd kill him and escape.

But he still loved his father. The love was mutual. But David and his younger brother were at odds, both wanting to take over the cartel once Arturo was gone. Not that anyone told her anything, but she'd been here two months. She could read the writing on the wall. There would be a war after the father was dead.

"It's hard to tell. A week, a month...He's got a strong will." That much was true, but she didn't think he'd last another week. The clock was ticking for her because once Arturo was dead, they had no reason to keep her alive. Unless they planned to keep her on as a personal doctor, but she didn't think so. Not when her specialty was oncology and was the entire reason she'd been kidnapped.

"I will miss him once he's gone."

Mary Grace didn't respond as they turned into another shorter, mosaic-tiled hallway. Exposed wooden beams criss-crossed the ceiling of this hallway as well, making the place seem even bigger than it was. Everything in the home was tile and wood, giving it a rustic feel. But it had all modern appliances and technology.

"He made me promise to let you go once he's gone," David continued. "I will keep that promise."

Mary Grace simply nodded because she didn't believe David. When Arturo had been talking and awake more than asleep, he'd taken a liking to her.

"You don't believe me?" His voice was rich and cultured but there was no surprise in the question.

"Of course I do," she said as they entered the kitchen. A big, fat lie.

"You do not lie well."

"I'll take that as a compliment." The scent of heavy spices filled the air and though she tried to fight it, a wave of nausea slammed through her. She couldn't make it to the nearest bathroom. Gagging, she raced for one of the sinks and began dry heaving. Only the water she'd had half an hour earlier came up, but she couldn't stop the shudders racking her body.

She was vaguely aware of a gentle hand rubbing her back. When she straightened, she wasn't surprised to find Jesus, the chef, looking at her anxiously.

"Sit." He was about five feet four and the kindest person in this place. But she knew better than to trust anyone here. She had no allies, no friends.

She did as he ordered, ignoring David's presence.

Jesus pulled out a Popsicle from the refrigerator. "I usually save these for *los niños*, but this will help with the morning sickness. I'll make you some ginger tea, then you need to rest. You can try crackers later." He didn't wait for a response, just moved to the pantry and started pulling out stuff.

"You're pregnant." For the first time she heard true surprise in David's voice.

No point in denying now. "Almost sixteen weeks." If her calculation was correct, and she was certain it was. She'd discovered she was pregnant after arriving in Mexico. She'd come to the country as part of a mission outreach program with a world health organization. She'd planned to cut her trip short, to ask a doctor friend to take over for her so she could return home, but hadn't had the chance.

The memory of the day she'd been taken was seared into her brain. She'd been working with two other doctors and a group of volunteers in a small village one of the doctors was originally from. He'd wanted to help out his hometown, which was why she'd volunteered to go in the first place. He'd been a brilliant doctor and a kind man.

Everyone had been gunned down in a savage act of violence. Everyone but her. She'd begged for her friends' lives, begged for the innocent civilians, but the man had said everyone had to die. Everyone had to think *she* was dead. They'd burned the village, burned all the bodies, gone completely scorched earth, then tossed her into a Jeep and taken her to the Ramirez compound. Almost every night she woke up in a cold sweat, remnants of gunfire and screams from her nightmares still lingering in her mind.

She hadn't had the chance to tell her husband she was pregnant either. Which was maybe a blessing. If he thought he'd lost only her it would hurt him, but if he knew he'd lost both her and their unborn child... No. It would destroy Mercer. Her huge, strong husband had a big, soft heart.

"I *will* keep my father's promise." There was a note of conviction in David's voice this time but she still didn't believe him.

Hell, maybe he believed he would let her live, but she couldn't afford to trust anything the man said. Not when he was responsible for keeping her here against her will. Away from her husband.

Instead of telling him she thought he was a liar, she said, "I'd like some prenatal vitamin supplements. I can let you know what kind."

"That will be no problem."

"Do you think it would be all right if I got some fresh air later?" They had two pools and at least thirty acres of ranchland. Occasionally if the circumstances were right—and the cartel wasn't on high alert—she was given a modicum of freedom. It was all an illusion but she needed to get out of the house. Needed to think. And pray.

He nodded once then paused as he pulled out his buzzing cell phone. He frowned at the screen, then after a short, muted conversation with Jesus, he left.

Mary Grace knew that whatever his decision was regarding her life, she wouldn't depend on his mercy.

Because sooner rather than later she had to make a break for it. Even if she failed, she had to try to save herself and her unborn baby. The best way for that would be on a horse-riding trip. If she only had to get away from one or two men, it was better than trying to escape a fully guarded home. No matter what, she had to try something. Her time was running out.

CHAPTER TWO

—You say bitch like it's a bad thing.—

Four days later

Skye Arévalo scanned the tourist bar of the gulfside Mexican hotel. Right on the ocean, the view was beautiful and the drinks were relatively cheap. Hell, everything here was cheap compared to the States. Not that she cared. She was here for one reason and one reason only. To find a particular pilot. Diego Martin. He was going to fly her getaway helicopter. Guy was apparently a drunk, but he could also fly out of tight spots. That was what she needed.

It didn't take long for her to find him, hitting on a middle-aged American blonde who was very clearly annoyed by his advances. Her arms were tucked into herself; she wasn't even turning her head to respond to Martin. But he couldn't take the hint.

No, he was leaning over trying to get a better view of her cleavage. Classy.

Skye slowly made her way through the throng of people at the bar. Wind from the Gulf of Mexico rolled over her bare legs, but the sun was warm and there were no clouds in the sky. A perfect day.

"Diego Martin," Skye said as she reached the bar, sitting down on the opposite side of the tall, wiry man in his early forties. She had no doubt it was him since she'd seen his picture and he was missing the pinky and ring finger on one hand.

As soon as Martin swiveled toward Skye, the other woman bolted, drink in hand. "I know you?" He didn't sound drunk, so that was good. She knew he was bilingual—so was she—but if he chose to speak in English that was fine with her.

"Nope." Sitting on the high-top bar stool, she turned so she was facing him completely—not even minding as he checked her out in a leering, full sweep. She'd worn shorts and a flowy tank top. Flowy so she could hide a blade against her back. Not that she'd need it with this guy. She was fairly certain she could take him in hand-to-hand combat. "But you know Juan Perez, and he owes me." Perez owed Skye big, and her using Martin as a pilot was only the tip of the iceberg for Perez's payback.

Martin paled and started to slide off his stool but she moved lightning fast, lifting her leg and slamming her heel between his legs against the chair.

She held his gaze, ignoring the stares from others in the bar. "Walking away from me is like walking away from your debt to Perez. He owes me and he's lending *you* to me as a favor."

"You're full of shit, *bruja*."

"First, I am a bitch, but I'm not full of shit. Call Perez. I'll wait." Once upon a time when she'd been an agent for the CIA, Perez had fed her information and she'd saved his ass on more than one occasion.

He wasn't really a good guy, but he wasn't bad either. He had a lot of legal business in the US, California specifically, but he also ran guns up the West Coast. She'd been able to look the other way when he gave her tips on potential terrorists. In her world, there was no good or bad, just shades of gray. And Perez, he was all right.

When Martin looked as if he might try to run, she gave him her most winning smile and pulled her foot back. It took him off guard, making her smile even wider. "*Please* run. I haven't had a good chase in a long time."

"You crazy, *bruja?*"

"Yes. Call Perez or you're going to find out how crazy I am."

He pulled out an old-school cell phone and flipped it open. She snorted at the sight and waved off the shirtless male bartender when he stepped in her direction. They wouldn't be staying much longer.

Diego cleared his throat as he held his phone up to his ear. She watched, probably too gleefully, as he spoke quietly to Perez. His tanned, weathered face grew paler and paler as the seconds ticked by.

After snapping the phone shut, he shoved it in his pocket and attempted to smile, though he looked a little green. "I apologize for calling you—"

"Save it. I want to make sure we're on the same page. You will fly me in and out of where I want to go with no questions asked, correct?"

His throat bobbed as he swallowed. "Yes."

She knew that Diego owed Perez big—because the fool had tried to steal one of Perez's cargo planes. Instead of killing Diego, Perez had cut off a couple fingers, beat the shit out of him and allowed him to pay off his transgressions. He'd also made some very specific threats regarding a certain part of Diego's anatomy, and everyone knew Perez always kept his word. Since Diego wanted to keep his dick attached, he'd do whatever Skye said.

She slid off her stool. "Good. We're going straight back to your place. You can pack a bag and then we'll head to your hangar."

He sat up straighter. "You want to go now?"

"No. We'll leave in a few hours." After sunset, and she wanted him to sober up even if he didn't seem drunk. He was sitting at a bar, with a beer in front of him, so he'd been drinking. "But I'm not letting you out of my sight."

He fell in step with her, avoiding drunk, dancing tourists as a steady thump of island music filtered through speakers. "Where are we flying?"

"Anywhere I want." No way was she telling him it was into the Coahuila region—aka Ramirez territory. Not yet. She'd wait until they were at the hangar. Because one of Perez's men would be waiting to fly with them. He'd make sure Diego didn't abandon her in the middle of Ramirez territory with no freaking getaway helicopter. Martin might be afraid of Perez, but the Ramirez cartel was scary as fuck too. She had to be cautious with this guy.

"What should I call you?" he asked as they stepped onto a sidewalk.

"Boss, boss lady, badass bitch. I don't care." She sure as hell wasn't going to tell him her real name. Even if Skye Arévalo wasn't listed as dead, she still wouldn't tell him her name. She'd faked her death six months ago, but before that she'd worked for the CIA. Using aliases was second nature to her. So were disguises, and she had one on now—with her brunette wig and contacts, it helped her to blend in better and made it less likely Martin would be able to ID her at a later date.

Coming out of hiding was a risk, but she had to do it. She didn't care for many people and had no family to speak of, but there was one man she loved. Loved so much she'd faked her own death to save him from a monster. Now someone he considered family had been kidnapped, so Skye couldn't look the other way.

Everyone thought Doctor Mary Grace Jackson had been killed in the violence of the Coahuila region when the Ramirez cartel decided to exert its power. They'd wreaked havoc and violence on a couple small villages who dared to stand up to them. And Skye had heard through the spy grapevine that an American doctor had survived. An American doctor who was a specialist in oncology. Considering Arturo Ramirez was dying of pancreatic cancer, Skye thought the tip had merit.

So here she was in a coastal town in Mexico, forcing a has-been pilot to fly her into treacherous territory so she could save a woman Colt Stuart considered a sister.

Because Skye had to do this for him. Walking away from Colt, faking her death, lying to him, making him grieve... It ate her up inside. It had been for his own good, and the hardest thing she'd ever done. But that didn't mean she couldn't do this for him. A man she loved more than anything. A man she'd give up anything for. But he'd never know it was her who'd saved his friend. She'd make sure of it. She'd get in, get the doctor to safety, and disappear again.

* * *

Oh no. No, no, no.

Mary Grace wiped her damp palms against her loose, cotton pants and glanced over her shoulder at the door to Arturo's bedroom.

The cartel leader was dead.

The only thing keeping her alive was gone. The majority of her time was spent in his room, keeping an eye on him, taking care of him, making him comfortable. She'd only been away from him for about half an hour to eat and now...he was gone.

She couldn't be certain, not without doing blood tests, but she didn't think Arturo's death was from the cancer. Rafael Ramirez, youngest son and all-around asshole, had arrived at the compound this morning and she'd seen him sneaking out of the bedroom right before she'd come back from a quick dinner of soup and crackers. She'd managed to avoid him seeing her, but she'd heard David and him arguing about many things that morning. They'd been speaking in Spanish but she understood every word.

Rafael wanted to make a move on some territory and David didn't. Rafael had accused his brother of being weak and unable to make the hard decisions. He'd told his older brother that they weren't letting her go either, that if they did they'd appear even weaker. He'd told David that getting married and having children had made him soft. Rafael had serious contempt for David and his family—and if she had to guess, he had a hard-on for David's wife.

Thinking of David as weak was stupid, considering Mary Grace had seen the guy kill more than one person without breaking a sweat. But Rafael was an absolute psycho, according to some of the household gossip she'd heard. There weren't many here who liked him, thankfully.

But he was still David's brother, so Mary Grace wasn't going to accuse Rafael of anything without proof.

Moving quickly, she grabbed a syringe and drew three vials of blood from Arturo's arm. She tucked them into a small carrying case along with all the notes she'd kept on his condition. She wasn't allowed internet access but they'd permitted her to type up notes on a laptop. Then they'd printed everything off for her so she could stay organized. She hadn't been allowed a phone and she'd never even seen one except the cell phones the guards used. Trembling, she weighed her options. She would have to go to David with what she suspected and ask him to test the blood. But it might not matter. He could kill her anyway. Heck, Rafael could kill her before she made it to David. He could say he'd caught her trying to kill their father...

Her heart rate kicked up as the endless possibilities ran through her mind. The man had shown up today unexpectedly. Maybe he'd been planning something like this all along. Kill his father, then kill his brother. Then... Nausea roiled inside her.

With her evidence in hand, she hurried to the bedroom door and peeked out into the hall. It was clear, and as far as she knew there were no cameras watching her. And she'd searched.

As she took a step onto the tile floor, the walls trembled. What the—

A loud boom sounded from somewhere outside.

An explosion. Holy crap, the place was under attack! It had to be another cartel or maybe some law enforcement agency attacking. She doubted the latter, but it was a possibility.

Hurrying down the hallway, she passed the same armed guard she saw every day coming from the direction of her room.

"Go to your room and stay put! We're under attack." He didn't bother waiting for her response as he spoke rapid-fire Spanish into a radio. He just assumed she'd comply.

She did as he'd ordered but not because she planned to stay put. This might be her only chance to escape. The sun had set an hour ago and if the men were fighting, she had a very, very slim window. She couldn't just sit around and jeopardize her unborn child by waiting to die.

She tossed the bag onto the queen-sized bed and pulled out a pair of navy blue scrubs. Her childhood friend Colt had once told her that wearing dark blue was better than black when sneaking around in the dark. The man should know, since she was pretty sure he was a spy now. Her sneakers were gray but that would just have to do. Once she was dressed she pulled her dark hair back into a bun, slung the bag over her body crosswise, and peeked out the door.

A guard at one end of the hallway had his back to her as he spoke into a radio. His words were too low to hear.

Moving on quiet feet, she eased the door shut behind her and walked sideways in the opposite direction. Her heart beat in her throat as she kept her eye on him. If he turned and saw her she wasn't sure what he'd do.

Once she reached the end of the hallway she ducked down the connecting one. Relief surged through her to find it empty but she knew that could change in an instant.

As voices trailed from somewhere nearby, getting closer by the second, a burst of panic jolted through her. She ducked into the second door on the left, not surprised it was a bedroom. Most of these rooms were.

This one was empty for now, but there were clothes draped over the back of a chair. She snatched up a small knife on the desk and moved to the nearest window.

Orange flames were visible through the sheer, cream-colored curtain. When she pushed it to the side a fraction, her eyes widened. One of the barns was on fire, horses were running wild and two vehicles were smoldering. It looked like a war zone down there.

This was her chance. Likely the only one she'd get.

She unlocked the window and pushed it open. Tensing for an alarm to go off, she shoved out a breath when nothing happened, and climbed out. Even if an alarm did go off, they had a hell of a lot more to worry about right now than her.

Sucking in the cool, night air she shut the window then hurried along the side of the stucco house, making her way toward the back. If the barn and vehicles near the front were on fire, she could only hope she could make it through one of the fields undetected while everyone was distracted.

Men were shouting and then another rumble shook the ground. She jolted back when an SUV about a hundred yards from her exploded, shooting straight up into the air. As the horses whinnied, terrified, she took off running toward a field.

There were more shouts now and she had no idea if they were directed at her. She didn't care. She just had to get out of here. She'd run into the countryside and hide. She just couldn't go back to that place. Her heart in her throat, Mary Grace sprinted through the knee-high grass, her shoes and pants getting wet from the earlier, rare rain.

At the sound of an engine revving behind her, a burst of adrenaline splintered through her. *Run. Run. Run.*

It was getting closer and closer. The tree line was close too. Only thirty yards now. She could at least have a chance if she could just make it—

The vehicle pulled up next to her, showering dirt and water all over her. Mary Grace braced for the bullets, the pain ripping through her flesh.

"Your husband sent me! Get in!" a female voice shouted, dragging Mary Grace out of her tunnel vision.

Mercer. He'd sent someone...

She turned and realized it was a small Jeep-looking vehicle slowing down next to her with the passenger side window down. A woman with a mask and night vision goggles covering her face was behind the wheel.

Without pause Mary Grace jumped into the passenger seat even though she immediately knew the woman was lying, despite that first thought about her husband.

Because if Mercer had known she was alive, he wouldn't have sent anyone. He'd have come himself. But if it meant taking a chance with this woman or the many men with guns behind them—who would very likely assume she'd killed Arturo, given the timing of this insanity—she was going with the woman.

"Strap in and hold this." The woman shoved what was most definitely a detonator at her. "Don't press anything yet." Her voice was clear because of the mouth hole in the dark mask.

Mary Grace strapped in and looked behind them, her heart about to burst through her chest. This was all too surreal and terrifying.

"I don't want to start out with a lie. Your husband didn't send me, but I'm still rescuing you and I'm going to get you home to him," she said as gunfire erupted behind them. The woman pulled out a cell phone and made a call.

She must have had an earpiece under the mask, because she didn't hold the phone up to her head. Two SUVs were hot on their trail, tearing across the countryside about a football field length away.

"Press the detonator now," the woman ordered as they burst through a cluster of trees. It was incredibly dark without the headlights on but clearly the woman could see where they were going.

Using the muted interior light of the vehicle, she pressed the little black and silver button and turned around to see what happened.

Her eyes widened as multiple bursts of fire erupted in a long line that wrapped around a huge portion of the property. "Heh. Let's see you follow me now, losers," the woman muttered, her voice a little gleeful.

"Who are you?" Mary Grace asked, grabbing the door handle to steady herself as they bounced along the uneven terrain. The woman didn't answer, just kept driving in silence.

Mary Grace's heartbeat was an erratic tattoo as they burst through the cluster of trees onto a dusty, makeshift road she remembered arriving on before being taken to the Ramirez property two months ago. They were a few miles away now but they'd still have pursuers even if she couldn't see anyone behind them.

"Are we meeting up with your team?" Mary Grace had worked in a war zone before and she knew how these things worked. Sometimes American citizens were kidnapped and special ops-types of guys were sent in to rescue them. Whoever this woman was, she was almost definitely an American and had to be working for someone.

Her unlikely savior didn't glance her way, just kept facing forward, NVGs in place as she made another phone call. Once she was through, she said, "There's a helicopter waiting for us, but it's just me. We're good to go."

"You did all that?" Mary Grace jerked a finger behind her even though the fireballs were no longer visible.

"I have a capacity for creating maximum damage when necessary. It's one of my best skill sets." The woman sounded pleased with herself even as she tucked her phone under her leg and drove like a bat out of hell through the darkness.

Mary Grace didn't respond, just fell back against the seat and placed a protective hand over her abdomen—even though she didn't allow herself to relax. Until she was in her husband's arms, she'd likely never relax again.

"Son of a bitch. Hang on tight. We've got company." The woman's voice was controlled as she took a sharp curve on the dirt road.

Looking behind them, Mary Grace saw two sets of headlights in the rearview mirror. Her stomach dipped. Even if this woman had rescued her, she wasn't sure how the heck they were going to get out of here alive when they were outgunned and outnumbered in enemy territory.

And in this part of Mexico, the entire province was enemy territory. The populace were just regular people trying to live their lives, but the cartels had everyone in a state of terror here. There would be nowhere truly safe for Mary Grace until they crossed the border.

CHAPTER THREE

—I believe in karma. I also believe in a good throat punch
when necessary.—

Skye didn't outwardly panic. She rarely did. But now anxiety had started to thread through her system.

"When we make it to the chopper, you're going to jump out and run. I'll be covering you. We should have a few extra seconds on these guys and I've got someone who'll be laying down cover for us." Or he was supposed to. But Perez's guy hadn't answered her two calls since she'd picked up Mary Grace.

"Okay." To give her credit, the doctor was holding it together well. She would have had to, in order to survive living in the Ramirez compound for the last two months.

With café au lait skin, dark eyes and a petite frame, Mary Grace would blend in well if they had to run on foot. Something Skye worried was a real possibility.

Even though the guys chasing after them had turned on their headlights, she didn't bother. Not with her NVGs. She was trying to remain as invisible as possible, as long as possible.

The dirt road was clear because almost no one from the two nearby towns had any reason to travel anywhere near the Ramirez compound. She knew the family had homes in a couple countries, including the States, but ever since Arturo

Ramirez had gotten sick they'd been holed up here. The mountainous region protected them, for the most part. "This is going to get bumpy." She slowed the vehicle and made a hard turn into a cluster of trees, driving over dirt, roots and other foliage. They were so close to the rendezvous point she could taste it. And that bastard Diego had better be there.

"Is that a helicopter?" Mary Grace asked even as Skye heard the familiar *whop whop* of the chopper.

"Yeah." She pressed her foot on the gas, her muscles tightening as they jerked over the uneven ground.

As they burst through the trees into a small grass clearing, the helicopter lifted off, moving higher and higher away from them. He flew west, passing over them, and she wanted to scream. But she couldn't lose her cool. Not in front of the woman she'd just rescued.

Maybe their pursuers would think they'd escaped in the chopper.

"That was our ride?"

Son of a bitch. "Yep." She continued driving through the clearing, planning to keep on driving until she could dispose of the vehicle and switch to the other one she'd secured.

"Well—"

An explosion tore through the air behind them. Skye jerked to a halt, stopping the vehicle and ripping her NVGs off. "Stay put." She jumped out and watched as the helicopter fell from the air, an orangey red ball of flames above the trees. Moments later, the sound of screeching metal filled the air, followed by another, louder explosion.

Good thing they hadn't been on board after all. *Thank you, karma.* That's what Martin got for trying to leave her behind.

Moving quickly, she opened the back door and pulled out two backpacks. "Okay, get out now."

When Mary Grace did and hurried around to meet her, Skye gave her one of the packs. "There are a couple MREs, a pistol, and a satellite phone in there. I need to see if our pursuers are still coming after us." And stop them if necessary. She handed the woman a pair of NVBs. The binos weren't as good as the goggles she was using, but they would do. "I want you to head that way," she said, pointing into the cluster of trees. "The binos have thermal capabilities so you'll be able to see. Keep moving through those trees until you reach the edge of the forest. It leads to another paved road. You'll cross over it. I've got an ATV waiting with keys in the ignition about twenty yards into the next cluster of forest. If I'm not back in twenty minutes, leave without me. I'd planned to drive northwest to an abandoned home but I can't give you detailed directions because it's more of a by-memory thing. So you'll just have to hide on your own. I've seen your resume so I know you're smart. If you have to move out on your own," she said as she pulled out a couple hand grenades, "call your husband to come get you. He'll have the right contacts and you'll be able to blend in if you have to hide out for a while. Just don't trust anyone."

"But—"

"No. Go." She put on her own backpack, grabbed her NVGs and headed in the direction of the downed helo.

Her legs ate up the distance quickly as she raced back across the clearing. Her adrenaline was surging now, giving her an edge. It took less than seven minutes for her to make it through the woods. Dwindling flames were visible through the trees as she neared the crash site but she couldn't hear any voices and she couldn't see any human movement through her NVGs.

Stepping out into the road she saw that the helicopter had crashed onto one of Ramirez's vehicles and sliced up the second SUV. Holy shit. Talk about awesome karma.

She wasn't going to stick around and find out if there were any survivors. If there were, they wouldn't be in any shape to come after her and Mary Grace. Moving fast, she retraced her steps. When she reached the first all-terrain vehicle she almost tossed a couple grenades in it to destroy it, but just in case anyone was out here lurking, she didn't want to alert them to her presence.

As she hurried in the direction Mary Grace had run, she paused when she saw a body lying prone next to a tree. Bending down, she cursed. No need to check for a pulse when there was a bullet hole through his head. Perez's man, killed by Martin no doubt. If Martin hadn't just died in the helicopter crash, she'd hunt him down for this.

She searched the man for any personal identifiers, stripped his weapons and headed out again. She just hoped Mary Grace hadn't left already.

After breaching the cluster of trees, she pulled the NVGs off and raced across the deserted highway road into another cluster of trees. It should be easy enough to disappear into the forest, especially since she'd mapped out an escape route in case Martin decided to double-cross her. *Always be prepared.* With the light of the half-moon it was easy enough to see her way through this part of the forest.

"Over here," Mary Grace whispered once Skye stepped around a big pine tree.

"We're safe for now," Skye said, hurrying to meet her, her boots crunching over fallen leaves and branches. As she stepped up to her, the sky rumbled overhead. It was supposed to be the freaking dry season but Mother Nature apparently hadn't gotten the memo.

She pulled out a raincoat poncho and goggles and handed them to Mary Grace. "Put these on." Then she pulled out her own goggles and moved her backpack around to her front side before sliding onto the small ATV. "You call your husband yet?"

Mary Grace got on behind her and wrapped her arms around Skye's waist. "No. I...want to more than anything. But if you didn't come back, I didn't want to call him only to be killed an hour or two later by the Ramirez cartel. He's too far to come get me and it would be beyond cruel to give him that kind of hope." Her voice cracked on the last word.

"He was right about you." Colt had told her all about his childhood friends, the six people he'd grown up with and loved as if they were family. He'd wanted to introduce Skye to all of them. Hell, he'd talked about them so much she felt as if she knew them. Only three of them—including Mary Grace—lived in Redemption Harbor now, but their friendship had stood the test of time and distance. He'd once told her that Mary Grace had a big heart. Too big and too soft was what he'd actually said. But he'd said it in that way a guy talks about a little sister who he worried about.

"Who?"

Ignoring the question and cursing her own stupidity for revealing any personal information, she started the engine. "This thing isn't too loud but sound can carry in places. Only talk if you have to. We've got about a two-hour ride through the forest. It'll be bumpy and uncomfortable. But we're getting a good head start."

"I'm ready to go. And thank you for saving me."

She didn't respond, just headed out into the moonlit night, the purr of the engine and the distant thunder the only noises. Skye hated that the first escape out of here had failed, but that was why she always had a backup plan. Usually two or three.

Always be prepared. That was her motto. And it was why she often carried explosives. Could never be too careful.

* * *

Skye guided the vehicle into the old barn and shut it off after parking it in one of the long-unused stalls where they'd be crashing for the night. The place had been abandoned a little less than a year ago when the old man who owned it had died. His daughter had left it and this small town for parts unknown. Texas, if Skye had to guess.

"We're safe here?" Mary Grace whispered.

"That's a relative word, but yeah. Sit tight for a couple minutes." She hurried to the next stall, grabbed the faded gray tarp and hurried back to cover the ATV. This farm was four miles from the nearest town, and from what she'd heard, people didn't venture here much. But she wanted to hide as much of their presence as possible. "Hope you don't mind sleeping on the ground."

"I'd rather sleep here than in that freaking mansion." Heat laced the woman's words.

"Did they…hurt you? Abuse you?"

Mary Grace shook her head as she stretched her arms over her head and twisted, working the kinks out of her body. "No."

"Good. If you want to, call your husband, tell him you're alive. We're heading out early tomorrow."

"Do you think we'll make it?" she asked, even as she pulled out the satellite phone Skye had given her earlier.

"I do. We'll be able to blend and I have a plan for getting us out of here in a few hours. I just need to make some calls, make sure we're still good to go."

"What should I tell him about you?"

"That I'm your guardian angel." Because Mary Grace's was clearly a slacker.

"Okay, but…"

"Just tell him I work for the US government and I'm part of a rescue team. The rest of the team was killed and I'm bringing you home. Final destination is Corpus Christi." She'd already hired someone who'd be able to get them across the border without alerting anyone. It would just be a matter of getting to the small, makeshift airport without anyone discovering them. "And honestly, I'd tell him to keep his mouth shut about this and maybe even hole up somewhere other than his home. Because if David Ramirez thinks you're alive, he'll send someone to check out your husband, to see if you've contacted him. I don't know the connections Ramirez has in the US, but I know he has them."

"Arturo Ramirez is dead. There's a good chance they'll think I poisoned him."

"Did you?"

"No."

"Okay. Even if you did, it doesn't matter to me. The guy was a piece of shit. But that puts another wrinkle in getting you home safely."

"He was dying of pancreatic cancer. Had maybe a month to live at the most. I had no reason to kill him. The longer I kept him alive, the better for me. He was the reason I was still alive at all. I think Rafael Ramirez, his youngest son, killed him. I saw him coming out of his father's room and then when I checked on Arturo, he was dead. I took blood samples, which are in my pack." She patted the small bag strapped across her middle. "And I took all the copies of his medical work. I can prove I had no reason to kill him. But the timing of your rescue and him dying…it doesn't look good for me."

The wheels had already started turning in Skye's head. "We'll make this work. I'll make it work with David Ramirez. It's not a stretch that Rafael would try to kill their father. And no one wants that psycho in power."

"Really?"

"Yeah. David will keep the region stable. His brother will wreak havoc."

"How do you even know that? And seriously, take off that mask. It's creepy."

Skye had kept her black mask on for multiple reasons, the main one being she didn't want Mary Grace to be able to identify her to anyone. Not Colt, not Mercer, no one. "First, I want your word on something. I think most people are liars, but I've heard from a reliable source that you have honor, so I want you to promise that you won't tell anyone what I look like. Not even your husband. I'm rescuing you as a Good Samaritan but I don't want anyone to know who I am or what I look like. So you won't speak of me once I've gotten you to safety. Agreed?"

"Yes, I swear it."

"If you're facing torture, you can tell someone who I look like." She felt like she needed to tack that on. Because Mary Grace seemed like the kind of person who'd try to hold out if she was being tortured.

Mary Grace blinked, then let out a rusty-sounding laugh. "Agreed."

She yanked off the mask, glad to have it off. It was made of cotton and breathable, but still uncomfortable for so long, especially for that long ride in the forest.

"What?" she asked as Mary Grace stared at her.

"I don't know. I expected you to have two noses or something. You're...stunning."

Skye gave a muted laugh and pulled the black rubber band out of her now messy ponytail. Her hair was long and auburn, courtesy of her mother's Scottish heritage. Her skin was a few shades lighter than Mary Grace's, courtesy of her father's Spanish heritage. "Well, back at ya, Dr. Jackson."

"You can definitely call me Mary Grace. And thank you again for saving me."

Skye lifted a shoulder. "Call your husband. And please tell him not to alert anyone. Not yet. It'll put us in danger."

Mary Grace nodded. "My husband is smart."

Yeah, well men did dumb things when it came to women they loved, but Skye nodded. As Mary Grace made the call, Skye stripped off the long-sleeved dark sweater she'd had on as well, needing to let her skin breathe a bit after that ride, despite the forty-eight degree weather. Dusting off her pants, she exited the small barn and conducted a quick perimeter check. The house was about fifty yards off and she wasn't going to bother doing a recon of it. There were no lights on and she'd hear someone coming anyway. She rarely slept, usually only in two- to three-hour batches.

After faking her own death she'd been lying low and trying not to think about—obsess over—Colt Stuart. It was incredibly easy to picture him in her mind. With dark hair, green eyes and a smile that made her panties melt, she would never forget the man. At thirty-four he was in his prime physically, muscular but not bulky. And she'd kissed every inch of his hard, toned body. Gah, that frustrating, sexy man filled most of her thoughts anytime she allowed herself to relax.

Walking away from him had been almost impossible. But she loved him too much to do otherwise. Because by simply existing, she was putting him and anyone he cared for in mortal danger. She wished it was different... *Nope, not going there.*

For the moment she shook off thoughts of him and leaned against the outside of the barn. Stars sprinkled the sky and a cool breeze rolled over the damp terrain, caressing her bare arms as she made her first phone call to the pilot she'd hired to fly Mary Grace back to the States. After letting him know he was on standby, she made another call as backup to a Border Patrol agent she knew, who'd also be able to help them get into Texas with no issue.

She didn't actually plan to go back to the US with Mary Grace. She just wanted to make sure the doctor was in good hands before she let her go and went her own way. If she had to, Skye would deliver Mary Grace to her husband, but she'd rather part ways before she got that far.

Once she was done, she headed back into the barn. Mary Grace was leaning against the tarp-covered ATV, wiping tears from her eyes. But Skye was pretty certain they were happy ones.

She held out the phone to Skye. "My husband wants to speak to you, if that's all right?"

Nodding, she took the phone. "Hello?"

"Ma'am…I don't know how to ever thank you, but thank you for getting my wife back to me." His voice was thick with tears, making her uncomfortable.

Skye had never dealt with crying men. Or kids. Both were scary. "No need to thank me. We head out in a few hours. Did your wife tell you to lie low?"

"Yeah, but I'm not sitting at home waiting. We'll meet you in Corpus Christi."

She wondered who the "we" was, but didn't ask. "Did she also tell you not to alert anyone—"

"Yes. I'm only telling a few trusted friends. They're all former military, and all of them have security clearances. Some higher than others."

"Okay." She had a feeling she knew who all those friends were as well, since Colt had told her about his friends, men he considered family. "We'll keep this phone for now. Your wife will call you as soon as we reach the airport she'll be flying out of."

"She?"

Hell. "I will personally be putting her on a plane with someone I trust. She will be returned home to you safe and sound." Skye didn't like making promises, but she damn sure intended to keep this one. For Colt.

"But you're not flying with her?"

"I hadn't planned to." Because she needed to have a sit-down with David Ramirez and that was going to take some particular finessing. If he didn't agree to let Mary Grace go free and clear, Skye would have to kill him. And his brother too, because that crazy bastard couldn't be allowed to take over the cartel. She might not be CIA anymore, but she still had a responsibility.

"I don't want her flying without you. She said you're her guardian angel, and she trusts you. What's the airport you'll be flying out of? I'll just meet you and take her myself."

Airport was a bit of a stretch. It was more like a landing strip in the middle of nowhere. "On the chance this call is being monitored—and I don't think it is—I'm not telling you." He'd never be able to find it anyway. Not without exact coordinates. "And it would take you a hell of a lot longer to get to it than it'll take for me to get her home. That's more time she's on Mexican soil."

Mercer cursed.

"I'll go with her to Corpus Christi," she said quickly, not wanting to drag this out any longer. They needed rest before setting out again. And she wanted to get out of here before daybreak. Much easier to steal a car in the early morning hours. Right now she was certain Ramirez would have people looking for them in any nearby towns. But the hour or two right before dawn, most people would be sleeping. That was when she'd make her move.

"Thank you. Mary Grace said your team died. I'm incredibly sorry for that. Was...a man named Colt working with you?"

Just hearing his name made her go still, but she answered quickly. "I don't know anyone by that name." And she hadn't technically had a team. She'd just told Mary Grace that in reference to the pilot and Perez's dead guy.

Mercer let out a breath. "Okay. Can I talk to my wife now?"

She handed the phone to Mary Grace so they could say their goodbyes. Soon enough they'd be on the road, on the way to freedom.

At least for Mary Grace. Skye wasn't sure she'd ever have true freedom. Not until a monster was dead.

Her only saving grace was that he thought she was dead. And she was hunting him, determined to eliminate him before he finally got someone to steal what he wanted. Something that could kill thousands upon thousands. If he discovered she was alive, however...

She wouldn't let that happen.

* * *

With a trembling hand, Mercer set his phone on the side table in the living room. He'd been sleeping—the times he could—on the couch in the living room the past two months because he hadn't been able to get in the bed he'd shared with his wife.

Mary Grace. Who was alive.

The woman he'd loved since he was fifteen was alive. And relatively unharmed. He swiped at tears he hadn't even realized had fallen. He wasn't a crier, but hell. Mary Grace had just called him.

He wanted to run right out the door and fly to Mexico. But that would be stupid. He had to formulate a plan and get to Corpus Christi. That was the first goal. Then if needed, he'd head right into Mexico and bring his wife home. But Mary Grace had assured him the woman who'd rescued her was a pro. So right now he had no choice but to trust that.

He nearly jumped as his phone buzzed, thinking it was Mary Grace calling or texting. When he checked the incoming text message, he stood.

"Everything okay?" Brooks asked, meeting him in the hallway as he appeared out of freaking nowhere. As if his buddy had been lurking. Which he probably had. The guy had been on him like a shutdown cornerback the past four days.

"Yeah. Savage is here"

"Wha—here, as in outside?" Brooks glanced at his watch. "At two in the morning?"

"Yeah. Called him a few days ago." Mercer had called another of their childhood friends because he'd been certain that Colt and Brooks were keeping something from him. Savage did contract work in places of the world most sane people wouldn't travel to, and it had taken him a few days to get back to the States. Now Mercer was glad he'd called. Because Savage and Brooks would be coming with him to get Mary Grace.

Without saying anything else, he headed to the front door and pulled it open.

With a tired smile, Zacharias Savage pulled Mercer into a tight embrace. Guy was one of his few friends who was as big as him, though unlike Mercer, he'd never played pro ball.

"Good to see you guys," he said, clapping him on the back before dropping a duffel into the foyer. Then he did the same to Brooks as Mercer shut the door.

"God, it's good to see you too. Can't believe you didn't tell me you were headed into town." Brooks shook his head slightly.

Of all of them, Brooks and Savage were closest to each other. Had been since they were teenagers. "I made him promise not to contact you," Mercer said, looking between the two dark-haired men. "Because I know you and Colt are keeping something from me. I asked him here so he could get it out of you. But as of three minutes ago I think I know what you've been hiding. I just got a call from Mary Grace. She's alive."

Silence reigned for a full five seconds until Brooks smiled and rubbed a hand over the back of his neck. "He found her. Thank God." Relief, joy and too many other emotions were in his friend's voice.

Mercer felt every one of them too. Joy the most prevalent. "No, he didn't. Some woman did. Mary Grace said she's kind of intense, blew a bunch of shit up and pretty much single-handedly rescued her. Definitely has training, though she didn't tell me much else, not even what the woman looks like."

"Colt went after her," Brooks said, confirming what Mercer had figured out by now. "He made me promise, because—"

"Yeah, I can guess why. If she hadn't been alive..." No. *No.* He was getting his wife back. Life couldn't be that cruel to take her away after this. "I'm still pissed at the two of you, but I'm gonna let that go for now."

"What's the plan?" Savage asked quietly, clearly not needing any other details.

Yeah, he loved his friends. "We pack bags and head to Texas. The woman who's got my Mary Grace said that's where she'll be bringing her. They'll be heading out in a couple hours. I'll tell you everything I know once we're on the road."

"I'm already packed," Savage said.

"I can be ready in five minutes," Brooks said.

"Same here." According to his wife, she'd been held by the Ramirez cartel to take care of the dying patriarch. Eventually Mercer wanted everyone who'd hurt his wife to pay, but for now all he cared about was getting her back and keeping her safe. "We need to get ahold of Colt too. You have a way to contact him?" he asked Brooks, already heading up the stairs to pack.

"Yeah. He's gone mostly dark, but he's been checking his messages and texting me to let me know his progress."

Mercer owed him. Big time. And he owed Mary Grace's mysterious savior. "Tell him we're on the way and someone else got to Mary Grace first." Even though she was safe for now, Mercer wouldn't be able to breathe easy until he held his wife in his arms again.

CHAPTER FOUR

—Blood makes you related. Love and loyalty make
you family.—

Colt stared at the prisoner he'd tied to a chair in this dingy
shack in the middle of nowhere, Mexico and ripped the
hood off his head. Even if the guy screamed, no one would
hear him. He'd picked a rural area to take this guy to instead
of an urban one. If by chance someone did overhear, it was
unlikely they'd call law enforcement. No, everyone here
avoided calling the police if possible. Everyone but tourists.
And he was definitely not that.

"*¿Inglés o español?*" he barked.

"English is fine," the guy muttered, anger and a little resignation on his face—as if he was preparing to be tortured.

Colt figured it would be English, considering Santiago
Lopez lived in Texas. Born in the United States, he'd been recruited by the Ramirez cartel at the age of twelve. Colt knew
that from one of the files he'd copied and taken before he'd
decided to undertake this solo mission. "You're going to tell
me everything I want to know about the missing doctor."

Lopez looked away from him, no doubt taking in his sur-
roundings, looking for a way to escape. They were in an abandoned home, likely of a poor farmer who'd either died or
headed to the nearest city. Probably the former. There was
nothing on the walls except a few framed photographs.

Threadbare furniture had been left as well, but everything of value was gone.

"I got no idea who you're talking about."

Colt reined in a sigh. He didn't have weeks to break this guy. Not when Mary Grace's life was on the line. "We can do a whole song and dance here where I torture the shit out of you and I'll never know if you're telling me the truth or not." He pulled out his SIG, strode toward the guy and pressed the weapon against his crotch. No time to finesse this situation. "Because torture rarely works. But I'll have to try, regardless, because I want to know about the individual who took the doctor."

Lopez shifted against the chair, struggling against his wrist and ankle bindings, but there was no give. Pressing a SIG up against a man's junk was almost a surefire way to get him to talk.

Colt pressed the weapon harder. "It's obvious I'm not a cop." He'd kidnapped the guy leaving a bar thirty minutes ago, thrown him into the trunk of a car he'd stolen, then brought him to this place out in the country. Colt had nothing to lose at this point. He had to find Mary Grace. For all he knew she'd been kidnapped by someone else. Doubtful, but he wouldn't rest until he knew she was safe.

"You're DEA," the man spat.

Colt snorted at that. "Not even close. As I was saying, I'll tell you what I want to know. You answer my questions or I unload a few well-placed bullets into your body, then leave, guaranteeing you endure an agonizing, drawn-out death. Before you tell me to fuck off, listen. I know David Ramirez was holding a female American doctor captive. I also know his father died yesterday—right around the time their compound was attacked, and now the doctor is missing. I give zero fucks about her." A complete lie. "I simply want to know who took her. You answer this, I'll let you go. You're not betraying your boss, you're not betraying anyone. So you tell me what I want to know, and you live. I call that a win-win."

Lopez shuddered, shifting against the chair again as sweat streamed down his temples despite the even temperature. Most of these guys who worked for the cartel were weak and uneducated. They were brave when they were in a group, but alone they were all out for number one. Lopez was no different. He might have loyalty to the cartel, but that only went so far. These guys weren't like the Russians—who were basically impossible to break. Those guys had a type of loyalty that Colt could respect.

No, this guy would talk. Colt could see it. "What's it gonna be?"

"I tell you what you want to know, how do I know you won't just kill me?"

"You don't know. But if you don't talk, or attempt to lie to me, I'll definitely kill you. And it will take a while. I have a gift for creating maximum pain." His voice was as hard as his expression.

His prisoner swallowed and gave a shaky nod. "Fine, fine. I wasn't there, but I've been out on patrol trying to find out who took the doctor. David ordered all of us to find the bitch who blew up the compound. His guys took out her getaway helicopter but she must have had a backup plan. No one can find a trace of either woman."

Colt hid his surprise that it was a woman. Using multiple maps and what he knew of the surrounding area, he'd drawn a grid, trying to figure out how far Mary Grace could be. Which was how he'd ended up here. "What did the woman look like?"

"No one knows."

He gritted his teeth, but the man shook his head quickly. "I'm serious. There were a few security feed images captured during their insane getaway. It was definitely a woman who was driving away with the doctor. But she had on a mask and NVGs. And according to the guys who were there, she was working alone. At least at the compound. She could've had backup but no one saw any until the chopper."

"You said the getaway helicopter was destroyed?" So whoever this mystery woman was had been working with someone. He could go from there and discover her identity. And discover it he would. He hadn't come this far only to fail. Not when a woman he loved like a sister was out there alone in cartel territory.

"Yeah. Our guys did it, but then the chopper crashed, taking out everyone. It was crazy."

"Who was the pilot?"

The man swallowed again, looked down at the weapon still pressing against his crotch, before flicking his gaze back to Colt's. "A nobody. Just some asshole, uh...Diego something. I don't know his last name."

"Think really hard." Colt kept his voice low, threatening. Right now he simply wanted to remind the guy who was in charge and get the truth.

"Ah...I don't know. I swear! He used to hang out at *La Bahía* down by the gulf, a few hours from here. Some gringo asshole who moved down here. There was another guy though. One of our guys found someone who'd been shot—not by us—who worked for Juan Perez. Not in the chopper but nearby. David recognized the guy, was pissed that one of Perez's men had been in his territory. It doesn't even make sense. It's not like they're rivals. Perez isn't into our trade."

Colt frowned at the name. Juan Perez, a legitimate businessman to the public, was into a lot of illegal endeavors—not drugs—but he had no known beef with the Ramirez cartel. And Perez had once had a relationship with Skye. Not a sexual one, that was for damn sure, but he'd occasionally fed information to her. Colt locked up thoughts of her. Now was not the time to get distracted. "You're sure?"

"Yes, yes! Can you move that fucking gun away now?"

Without moving a fraction, he asked, "What are Ramirez's plans for the doctor?"

Now that David's father was dead he'd be taking over the cartel. He shouldn't have a reason to go after Mary Grace. Not unless he considered her a loose end for whatever reason, or if he thought she'd killed his father. Colt couldn't see her killing anyone, but she'd been a captive and would have done anything to survive. If he knew one thing about human nature, it was that people surprised themselves when trying to stay alive. Still, he couldn't see her killing a man dying of cancer. Her being on American soil wouldn't matter to David Ramirez either, if he thought she'd killed Arturo. He'd send someone after her if he viewed her as a threat, or for vengeance. He'd have to save face and kill her if he thought she'd murdered his father.

"How should I know? I saw that bitch once! She was inside the compound most of the time."

And Lopez wasn't the kind of guy who got invited into the privacy of the Ramirez compound. He was just a low-level asshole. A nobody. But even he knew things. "Yet Ramirez has you and all his guys out looking for her and her rescuer."

"Well, yeah. He's going to kill the other bitch once he hunts her down. I don't know what he wants with the doctor. Who the hell cares?"

Colt nodded once and withdrew his weapon from the guy's crotch. Lopez let out a sigh of relief and that was when Colt struck out, slamming his fist against the guy's jaw with a sharp, brutal punch. The prisoner didn't have time to react, just took the force of the punch, his head lolling back as he lost consciousness.

Wincing at the pain in his knuckles, Colt ignored it as he tucked his weapon away with his other hand.

It was doubtful this guy would tell anyone he'd talked to Colt, because he would put a spotlight on himself if he did. And while he might deny that he'd said anything, David Ramirez wouldn't believe it. Because Lopez had been tied up, at Colt's mercy. And he was physically unharmed for the most part. They'd think he was a snitch. Nah, this guy wasn't saying anything. But Colt was still leaving him tied up here. The asshole could get out of the bonds himself or die trying.

Sliding his sunglasses over his eyes, Colt stepped out of the house, saw nothing but a patch of unplowed farmland.

Pulling out his cell phone, he strode toward his stolen car. Over ten years old, not flashy, it had a good engine and helped him to blend in when on the road.

Brooks picked up on the first ring, as if he'd been waiting. Colt got straight to it. "There's been a—"

"I'm with Mercer and Savage. We're on our way to Corpus Christi."

Before he could ask what the hell was going on, and when Savage had gotten into town, there was a short rustling sound right before Mercer got on the line.

"Mary Grace is alive. I spoke to her. She's with an unknown woman who's promised to bring her back to me. She was part of some government rescue team. They're supposed to fly into Corpus Christi, which is why we're headed that way."

Colt frowned. That was more information than he had on the rescuer. But there hadn't been any sanctioned rescues that he was aware of. "What do you know about the woman?"

"Almost literally nothing, except that she saved Mary Grace. I don't even have her name. She wanted to just put Mary Grace on a plane but I made her promise to fly in with her. She said she would."

"How's Mary Grace?" he asked.

"She sounded good. In good spirits, at least. I want to be there right fucking now."

Yeah, Colt could imagine how helpless the guy felt. "I know."

"You should've told me you were going after her."

He slid into the driver's seat and started the ignition, glad when it purred to life. He didn't pull out of the driveway yet though, not until he knew which direction he was headed. "We'll agree to disagree. Do you know where they're flying out of?" Colt figured it was doubtful, because if the woman was trained enough to get Mary Grace out of the Ramirez compound, she wasn't going to be flying commercial.

"No. I know nothing, not the time or the actual airport or...nothing. I'm assuming it's private."

Yeah, no doubt. There were a few private airports in and around Corpus Christi too. "You got a phone number for her?"

"Yeah."

"Text it to me. I'll see what I can do with it." Colt wouldn't be able to use his resources at the CIA since he was most definitely not supposed to be in Mexico right now. His boss thought he was on vacation, so he'd be in a shitload of trouble if the higher-ups found out what he was up to. He'd gone completely off grid. And he didn't care.

Mary Grace and Mercer might not be his blood, but that didn't matter. They were family, and he would go to hell and back for his family.

Knowing he was going to catch hell from the man he called next, he braced for it as he dialed the number from memory.

"Yeah?" Gage Yates, one of his childhood friends—who'd also grown up with Mercer and Mary Grace—answered on the second ring. Gage worked for a private security firm handling most of their cybersecurity. Guy was a genius, and had been headhunted by the government on multiple occasions. But private paid better, and Gage lived in shades of gray— even if he had been in the Corps years ago.

"It's Colt."

"Hey, asshole. Hear you decided to go all rogue and not tell any of your friends that one of their best friends might be alive."

He winced at the raw anger in Gage's voice, because it was warranted. "You want to do this now, or you want to help me track Mary Grace?"

"What do you need?" His voice was all business now.

"Got a phone number Mary Grace called Mercer from."

"Yeah, already got that from Brooks."

"You tracing it?"

"Yeah. Thing's bouncing all over the place. I can't get a lock on it." Frustration laced his voice.

"*You* can't?" Gage had been hacking since he was a teenager. When it came to computers, the man was a genius. There was a reason he'd been intel in the Corps, and that the NSA, CIA and other various government acronyms headhunted him on a consistent basis.

"Damn it, no."

"I need you to run information on a man named Juan Perez." Since the name was common enough, Colt gave him the man's stats. "I don't know that he's involved directly, but one of his guys was found dead at the scene of the helicopter crash." He was assuming Mercer had given Gage everything he'd told Colt, so didn't bother explaining everything he knew. "I can't see him going up against the cartel, but see if he's got any properties in the area. Run a two hundred mile radius moving out from the Ramirez cartel's province." It was likely too big but he didn't want to miss anything. "And see if there's been any chatter about two women—"

"Dude, already running that. Give me a sec..." Which turned into five minutes—while Colt sat there counting every second.

He was used to having the Agency's resources at his fingertips, being able to call for backup at the drop of a hat. He didn't always get it, but there was almost always someone else on the other end of the line able to help him with information. And information was gold when out in the field like this.

"All right. He—and by he, a shell corporation that I can trace back to Perez—owns a few properties in the region. Where are you at now?" When Colt told him, Gage let out a low whistle. "He owns a warehouse about fifteen miles from you. Not exactly urban, not rural either. Right on the outskirts of the next town over from you. The place is supposed to be for storing and shipping textile stuff. I'm texting you all the addresses though."

"Thanks. Look, I know all the local airports." Both legal and the ones that were basically airstrips used for illegal drug running. "Can you do a search and see if there are any connections to Perez at any of them?" It was a long shot but he hadn't been prepared for someone else to rescue Mary Grace. And since Perez had a connection to the mystery woman rescuer, he had to follow up on it.

"On it now."

Colt knew he was asking a lot of Gage—who was most definitely working at his regular job right now. But he was going to ask even more. "I know this is a stupid question, but can I count on you for more backup if I need it?" Colt had other people he could call, assets mainly. Gage was the only person he could call who was truly a friend. Someone who wouldn't expect a favor for the information he was giving.

"Shut the fuck up. You better call. I'm available 24/7. And as soon as our girl is back, I'm heading to Corpus Christi too. But I'm here for you. All of you. I'll text or call when I get a ping on Mary Grace's phone."

Yeah, he should have expected nothing less. "Thank you. And I'm going to get her." After disconnecting he read the incoming text from Gage, plugged the nearest address into his GPS map. It was a long shot, but if someone was on the run, hiding from the Ramirez cartel and looking to lie low before heading out of the country, maybe they were using one of Perez's properties. The connection was there and he couldn't afford to overlook it. And it was the only lead he had.

CHAPTER FIVE

—Sweet baby pandas.—

"Do you need anything?" Skye asked quietly as she texted an asset—using one of her former aliases, which was a risk. But they needed yet another way out of the country because the makeshift airport they'd gone to had been crawling with Ramirez's guys.

She'd seen through her binos that her pilot was fine and none of Ramirez's men had been holding a weapon on him, so she assumed they'd just stopped at it because, hello, it was a freaking airport. Of course they'd check it out. They'd be morons not to. And from what she knew of Ramirez, he'd likely leave someone behind to watch the place. She could easily move in and kill a guard, but that would mean her pilot would become a target so she couldn't do that.

"I'm good." Mary Grace paced back and forth, stress vibes rolling off her in practically tangible waves.

"You should sit or something." Mary Grace hadn't stopped pacing since they'd arrived at the empty warehouse.

Instead of remaining out in the open they were in a boarded-up office on the second floor. Streams of light broke through the slats of the hastily nailed-in boards. A cheap desk was covered in a thick layer of dust and the metal filing cabinets were rusted out, but Skye had cleaned up one of the metal chairs so Mary Grace could sit.

"You think walking is bad for me and the baby?" Mary Grace lifted an eyebrow, faint amusement in her gaze.

Skye shrugged, a little defensively. "I know zero about pregnancy. I think you should be sitting or something though." Slight terror had invaded her veins when Mary Grace had told her she was pregnant on their drive here. She'd only told Skye because she'd gotten sick earlier and admitted it was because of morning sickness. Skye didn't understand the term "morning sickness" because it seemed like Mary Grace got it all the time.

"Well I'm the doctor. I'm good."

"If you say so." Skye eyed her carefully before looking at her phone again.

"I do. So what's the deal? We getting out of here soon?"

"Just waiting on a return call from a guy."

"A guy? Care to elaborate?" Mary Grace asked politely.

Skye wasn't used to answering to anyone, and especially not to a civilian, but she understood the other woman's need for information. The doctor was holding up incredibly well for all she'd been through. Had to respect that. "A guy who knows a guy who might be able to get us out of here through other means." And if he didn't return her text in a timely manner she'd reach out to her Border Patrol friend. Which she didn't want to do, but to get Mary Grace out of here, anything went right now. She'd inadvertently gotten one of Perez's guys killed, so Skye wasn't going to him—even if she was using one of his warehouses as a hideout.

"So…what should I call you?" Mary Grace asked.

"Raven is fine." Skye moved to the nearest window and peered through one of the slats. A few prostitutes lingered on the street as well as their pimp and a drug dealer, but she didn't see anything else out of the ordinary.

"You like the bird?"

She glanced over to find the doctor was finally sitting down. "What?"

"Well I know Raven isn't your real name."

She lifted a shoulder. "Oh, I like X-Men. Raven is Mystique's given name."

The doctor laughed slightly. "I thought she was a villain."

"She's complicated." Glancing out the window again, Skye frowned when she spotted an SUV pulling up to the curb out front. Could be nothing, but it was a nice, new vehicle. The kind that tended to stick out in this region of Mexico. It often signaled a narco. Not always, but the chances were good.

"People usually are."

"Yeah, sometimes." But most of the time the people she dealt with were predictable, greedy assholes. Of course, those weren't the people she fought for, made sacrifices for.

"David Ramirez said he was going to let me go. At first I didn't believe him, but he discovered I was pregnant. I think he at least thought he'd let me go. I don't know if he would have."

"Maybe." Skye looked at the woman again. She might be keeping it together, but there were circles under her dark eyes. "He'll likely want you dead now. Because he'll assume you killed his father."

"I know." She rubbed a hand over the back of her neck.

"I might know a way to convince him otherwise. I'll need your records and a vial of the blood you took."

The doctor's eyes widened. "You can't mean to meet with him."

Skye didn't answer, just looked out the window again to see a prostitute getting inside the SUV. *Okay, not a threat.*

At a subtle scuffing sound and a tingling sensation at the back of her neck, she turned to Mary Grace and held up a finger to her mouth. Then she motioned for her to hide behind the desk. Withdrawing one of her pistols, Skye moved on silent feet to the door of the small office. She peered out a small, glassless window. She couldn't see anyone on the dusty floor below, but that didn't mean anything.

Her instincts were almost never wrong. And they were telling her that she and Mary Grace weren't alone. Ramirez's guys were thugs though; they'd have made a shitload of noise if they'd broken into the warehouse.

So this could be one of Perez's men. Or maybe just some junkie looking for a place to crash.

Weapon up, she eased the door open, swept out onto the catwalk that looked over the bottom floor—and came face to face with the man who'd haunted her dreams for the past six months.

Ah, hell. She sucked in a breath as if she'd been kicked in the solar plexus. *Colt love-of-my-life Stuart.*

They faced off with each other in total silence, their pistols aimed at each other. He blinked, recoiled, then tucked his weapon away at the same time she did.

"Colt," she whispered, not sure what else to say as she stepped back into the room, mainly because he was advancing on her with too many emotions on his face to read.

The pain and anger though—yeah, she saw those. And they sliced her up.

"Oh my gosh, Colt!" Mary Grace popped up from behind the desk, but Skye kept all her focus on the tall, sexy and very, very angry man in front of her. "He's my friend," Mary Grace continued.

"I know who he is," she whispered again, unable to completely find her voice. How the hell had he found them? Damn it, she'd done some covert checking and he was supposed to be on vacation right now. Somewhere warm with his toes in the sand.

"You're alive? You're *alive?*" he growled at her, advancing like a predator, apparently not caring about anything else.

Her heart stuttered. "Colt—"

He was on her in an instant, his mouth crushing to hers as he threaded his hands through her hair, cupping the back of her skull in a tight grip as he kissed her, hungry, demanding. She gave in to it because this was Colt and she'd gone without his taste for way too long. She bit his bottom lip, moaning into him right before he savagely pulled back from her, putting a solid foot of distance between them. Breathing hard, he stared down at her, his chest rising and falling erratically, his expression one of utter betrayal.

He opened his mouth once, snapped it shut, then turned away from her, raking a hand through his military-short dark hair. He had a little facial scruff going on though, and damn, it was sexy. Everything about him was. Seeing him ripped off the pathetic little Band-Aid she'd put on her heart when she'd faked her death, leaving behind him and the life they'd started to create. The joy at seeing him in person, being able to touch him, battled with the terror at what this might mean for him now that he knew the truth.

"Mary Grace," Colt murmured, moving around the desk at the same time the other woman did. "Are you okay?"

"I'm more than okay." She went into his arms for a hug and he squeezed tight. "I can't believe you're here." Stepping back, he looked down at Mary Grace, and Skye drank in every mouthwateringly sexy line of him. Over six feet, no fat on him anywhere, he was hard and muscular, though he seemed leaner than the last time she'd seen him.

"We're going to get you out of here..." He turned to Skye again, his jaw tightening and his eyes turning to ice. "You better have a damn good reason why you faked your fucking death!"

She hated seeing the coldness in his expression but locked down her own emotions. They didn't matter. "Colt, we can't do this right now. We've got to get out of here, get her on a plane."

He stalked back to her until they were toe to toe. "I've been mourning you until this very moment. Tell me why you did this."

The guilt almost smothered her, making it difficult to drag in a full breath. "I can't." Because if she did, the man who wanted her dead would go after Colt. He'd rip apart Colt, his family, anyone Colt loved. Because that monster would want to hurt her. She had no one, so he'd been unable to threaten her family. But he had been able to target Colt. With her dead, he'd had no reason to go after Colt. Considering her tormentor had been close to Colt and was just as trained as she and Colt were, she hadn't been willing to risk the life of the man she loved. So she'd done what she'd had to.

Colt rolled his shoulders once, his expression harder than she'd ever seen it. "Oh, you'll tell me. First we've got to get Mary Grace out of here. I've got a pilot on standby about fifteen minutes from here."

She let out a small sigh, glad she wouldn't have to reach out to her Border Patrol contact. She'd also have to let her other contact know his services weren't necessary, but only after she saw Mary Grace and Colt get on a plane. Skye turned to Mary Grace, who was watching her with wide eyes. "Tell your husband I'm sorry I didn't fly with you to Corpus Christi, but I'll stay until you get on the plane. Colt will make sure—"

"If you think for one second I'm letting you out of my sight, you're out of your mind." Colt's voice was quiet, deadly. "We're going to get on that plane with her *together*."

No way. "I can't. David Ramirez thinks she killed his father. I'm going to set up a meeting with him." David might be scum, but he wasn't a psycho. He was still a businessman and he had to know that Mary Grace had nothing to gain and everything to lose by killing Arturo. Still, Skye wanted to meet with him, give him all the info Mary Grace had saved, including the vials of blood.

Colt let out a curse, turned away from both of them and rubbed a hand over his head. He'd always done that when he was trying to figure out the best plan of action. A moment later he swiveled back to face them. "We'll put her on the plane together. My pilot will get her to Corpus Christi, no problem. You and I will set up a meet with Ramirez together."

"Not happening."

"You need backup."

"No, I need you to use your head." Apparently he was determined to piss her off.

"Oh, I am. You're not leaving my side. If you do I'll broadcast your whereabouts to every US government agency."

She narrowed her eyes. "You wouldn't."

"Try me."

She didn't think he actually would, but she'd never seen him like this. "I should put a bullet in you right now, you stubborn jackass."

"Good. I'll have a scar to match the last time you stabbed me," he snapped, his big body vibrating with anger.

"That was in training and it was an accident!"

"Sweet baby pandas, you two are insane," Mary Grace muttered. "Can we please get the heck out of here now?"

"Yes," Skye said. "And stop stressing her out, she's growing a person inside her!"

Colt practically jumped as he turned toward his childhood friend. "You're pregnant?"

Mary Grace nodded, gave a hesitant smile. "Three months."

He cursed again, then started pulling his short-sleeved, sand-colored tactical shirt off. It took Skye all of two seconds to realize what he was doing.

Her chest squeezed when he pulled off his bulletproof vest and handed it to Mary Grace. Of course he would do that, because his heart was so damn big. "It'll be large on you, but put it on under your shirt."

"Colt, I can't take this." Mary Grace shook her head. "You need it."

"I'll step out while you change." His green gaze snapped to Skye. "And you're coming with me."

She wasn't intimidated by him. Just worried about what he'd do now that he'd found out she was alive. He wouldn't tell anyone, but he was likely to do something stupid. Like try to help her or not let her go, putting himself in danger.

Because arguing would be pointless and they needed to get the hell out of there, Skye went with him. "You can come with me," she said as they stepped out onto the catwalk. "But you can't let anyone know I'm alive. Mary Grace said she won't tell anyone what I look like, and she doesn't know my real name. When I meet with Ramirez I'll change up my look." Being this close to him was pure torture, a reminder of what she couldn't have.

"First, you're not meeting with him. I am. Second, what the fuck? Seriously, what the ever loving *fuck?*" The pain in his eyes made her glance away, out over the stale nothingness of the warehouse floor.

She was weak for not being able to witness all that raw emotion, but he'd made her weak from the moment they'd met. All cocky and obnoxious and...hers. God, their first time had been after a mission in some remote hut in the jungle. It had been wild, intense, and she'd never been able to get enough of him. He'd gotten into her system, into her blood, and he was it for her. Walking away from him once had almost killed her. Doing it a second time surely would. But if it kept him safe, it was worth it.

Mary Grace pulled the door open, adjusting her shirt over the vest, which was indeed too big on her small frame. "Hopefully I won't need this thing, but I'm ready."

"Good. What are you guys driving?" he asked.

"Stolen vehicle," Skye said.

"Me too. My guy knows what I'm driving, so we'll take mine. Mary Grace, you can lie in the back seat and...you'll be in the front," he said to Skye, carefully avoiding her name. Something she was grateful for.

It didn't take long to get to his car and load up. Skye didn't want to drag him into this with her, but if she argued it wouldn't go well. He'd just follow her, so they'd have to meet with Ramirez, make sure Mary Grace was safe from misguided revenge, and then she'd convince Colt to let her go. And not tell anyone she was alive.

"This is surreal. I never thought I'd see Mercer again. Thank you guys," Mary Grace said from the back seat as Colt steered onto the road.

"He's been a mess without you," Colt murmured, ever alert as he scanned the other drivers on the road.

"I would have been a wreck if I'd thought he was dead too."

Skye winced and looked out the window. The small town flashed by her in a blur as he drove. Though she knew she should be focusing, the neutral-colored buildings, some with graffiti, all flew by, blending into a blur of colors and shapes. There was a cartel war going on now and the criminal activity in this region was on an epic level. But it was clear Colt was sticking to the main roads, which should keep them relatively safe. Trickles of rain started drizzling against the window, the patter smarter to focus on than the man beside her.

"Why'd you go after her?" Colt asked a few moments later.

As if she was a puppet and he controlled her strings, Skye turned to look at him. "I remembered her name from all the stories you told me. Her death, along with all those doctors and civilians, made the news. I wasn't sure if it was even true, if she was alive, but I got a tip that the cartel had a female doctor from that massacre still alive..." She paused. "I wanted to do this for you. I know how much she means to you."

"Damn it. You make me crazy. I've literally never wanted to simultaneously fuck and shake sense into someone."

She looked out the window again. "You were never supposed to know."

He grumbled under his breath as he took another turn. "What airport are we headed to?"

"Not a real one. And we're using my friend's plane."

"Friend, or asset?" Skye asked.

"Friend."

Well, that made a difference. And if Colt trusted the pilot to get Mary Grace to Corpus Christi, she would too.

"So...you're definitely CIA, Colt," Mary Grace said from the back, breaking through the awkward silence after a couple minutes. "I freaking knew it. I knew you weren't an accountant! That's the lamest cover ever." Before either of them could respond, she continued. "And you, whatever your name is, you faked your own death? That's Lifetime movie kind of stuff. But if you did it, I'm sure you had a good reason. You should go easier on her, Colt."

Colt frowned. "What the hell, MG?"

"She saved my life because she knew what I meant to you. Pretty sure I'm going to make her my new best friend. I'm also pretty sure Mercer is going to kick your ass for not bringing him down here with you."

"He already got in a few good shots before I left."

Skye didn't respond, just listened as the two of them continued to banter back and forth. Their conversation was ridiculous but she understood that Mary Grace probably needed to talk or go crazy. She'd be on a plane to see her husband soon, and had to be close to her breaking point. Skye knew that once Mary Grace saw Mercer, once she was safe on American soil, she'd probably let go of any and all control. She'd probably end up sleeping for days.

A tiny part of Skye was actually jealous of that. She didn't have the luxury to let go.

When Colt turned down another road, mountains stretched out far in front of them, but not a soul in sight. "We're close," he said.

Skye automatically tensed, pulling out her weapon even though there was no danger to be seen. They were so damn close to getting the doctor off to safety, she didn't want to let her guard down.

"Is everything okay?" Mary Grace asked, her voice tight. Even though she was lying down, she still had a decent visual of Skye and Colt in the front seat.

"We're good. I'm just being prepared."

Skye scanned the rocky, mountainous expanse of land as Colt turned down another road. As they neared the turnoff into a warehouse that boasted a huge sign for helicopter rentals, she frowned. "I thought you were flying her into Corpus Christi." A chopper wouldn't make it that far.

"You can sit up now," he said to Mary Grace, who instantly popped up. "And my guy—Brooks's father's pilot—will get you across the border into Laredo. From there he'll fly you into Corpus Christi via plane. I wanted to get you across the border and onto American soil the quickest way. This will only be a forty-five minute flight, and then you'll officially be in the

US. This company isn't bothered by anyone because of...reasons."

Skye nearly snorted, not needing him to explain. No doubt whoever ran this company helped out the US and Mexico alike. They probably ran illegal shit into the US, and helped the US out by giving information on drug runners, but she didn't care as long as the pilot got Mary Grace to safety.

As Colt steered into a parking lot with only two vehicles in it, Skye zipped up her light parka and twisted her hair up before pulling on a plain ball cap. Then she slid sunglasses on despite the overcast day. "You want me to come with you?" she asked as he parked.

"No, I'll make sure she gets on. And if you leave without me, I'll hunt you down." He tossed the words over his shoulder without bothering to look in her direction as he got out of the car.

She knew he meant every one of them too. Even though she was tempted to leave, she couldn't do that to him. Not now. It would be stupid and unnecessary. Especially since she needed to convince him to let her remain "dead."

Taking her by surprise, Mary Grace lunged at her from the back seat, giving her an awkward hug from behind. Skye patted her arm, feeling uncomfortable. She didn't have many female friends. Only a couple really. And overall, she didn't have many friends, period. And her family hadn't been huggers. "Stay safe."

"Thank you," Mary Grace murmured. "Once you and Colt fix what's between you, you're coming to meet my husband. And he's going to feed you more food than you can imagine." She squeezed tight one more time before sliding out of the back seat.

Skye watched as her new friend and Colt hurried into the wide open rolling door of the hangar, disappearing from sight—and wondered what the hell she was going to do about this thing with Colt. Because even once they straightened out this mess with Ramirez—and she was hopeful they would—she wasn't sure how the hell to convince him to let her walk away.

Deep down, she wasn't sure she was strong enough to do it again.

CHAPTER SIX

—If she doesn't scare you a little, she's not the one.—

Colt was walking a dangerous edge as he drove with Skye through the mountains. They hadn't said much over the past couple hours, though he wanted to. He wanted to grill her about where she'd been, why she'd lied to him and who the hell wanted to hurt her. Because there was no way she'd have faked her death without a damn good reason.

Yeah, he was pissed, but he knew she still had a reason. And he was going to hear it.

"You have contacts with Ramirez?" Skye was the first to speak since watching that helo lift off, Mary Grace safely onboard.

"No. I'm going to reach out to him myself."

"We're doing this together," she snapped. "I started this, and I'm finishing it. Where do you want to hole up?"

"I've got a safe house about ten miles from the outskirts of the compound. But we're not going there. He'll be gone by now."

"How do you know?"

"Chatter."

"Where is he?"

Colt lifted a shoulder. If he didn't tell her, she couldn't run from him. And he wasn't certain she wouldn't do just that when the time was right. He wasn't losing her a second time.

"Seriously, you're not going to tell me?"

He shot her a sideways glance before turning back at the road. Looking at her almost hurt. Her long, auburn hair was pulled back in a tight braid against her head. Since they'd left Mary Grace she'd pulled it out from her ball cap and just had on sunglasses. It didn't matter that he couldn't see her eyes— he knew what they looked like, had stared into them as she'd ridden him, as he'd ridden her. It had been six months since she'd "died."

Six months he'd been in agony.

"You're so frustrating," she muttered as she double-checked the weapons she had strapped to her person, including her pistol, a couple blades and a bit of C4 tucked into one of the pockets of her cargo pants.

"You get any sleep last night?" he asked.

"Not much."

Yeah, he understood that. On missions, sleep was fleeting. Especially a mission where someone's life was in your hands. "Grab some shut-eye. We've got a couple hours' drive."

"You don't want to grill me?" Disbelief laced her voice.

"Oh, I will. But we'll do it on even footing." And not until he'd settled down first. "Get some sleep," he ordered.

She rolled her eyes but released the lever and leaned the seat back a few inches. Eyes closed, she murmured, "I'll sleep because I want to, not because you ordered me to."

He fought a grin. God, that was his Skye. His pretty little liar. With a unique heritage, her skin had a soft olive glow year-round, as if she was a perpetual beach bunny. In reality she hated beaches or even relaxing. Her idea of a vacation was... Well, what she'd just done at the Ramirez compound. A complex woman raised by spies, who'd both died in the field. He'd only found that out after a couple months of sleeping with her.

And she'd kept him at arm's length for those first couple months, only committing to monogamy but not much else. He'd known he'd get under her armor, get into her blood just like she was in his. Or he'd been determined to try. Apparently not determined enough, since she'd ghosted on him.

Only a few minutes passed before she fell asleep and he had to admit he was surprised. But she had to know she could trust him. He'd rather eat a bullet than hurt her in any way. It was the only reason she was allowing herself this vulnerability. And she had to be exhausted. Pulling off the kind of rescue she had with little to no resources—and he was just guessing, because she hadn't even been wearing a vest—was tiring. Working with no backup... He'd been like that before her.

And he'd charged down here to save Mary Grace without backup too, reverting back to who he'd been before Skye. Because the thought of working with anyone but her had been unbearable.

At least he'd done something right. Mary Grace was as safe as safe could be. Thirty minutes later he received a text from the pilot that they'd landed and were headed to Corpus Christi. Then he received another text from Mercer telling him that they'd heard from Mary Grace and would be seeing her soon. It was apparent from the text that Mercer was annoyed Colt wasn't with Mary Grace, but he had to do this for MG to make sure this didn't follow her home.

"Everything cool?" Skye asked without opening her eyes, her breathing still as steady as it was when she was sleeping.

"Yeah. MG's in Laredo, headed to meet Mercer now."

"Good. I like her. She's got a lot of spirit."

"Yeah, she does." Kind of like another woman he knew. He wouldn't rest until he knew Mary Grace was with Mercer, however. "So what's this threat you're facing?"

"What makes you think I'm facing anything?" Her voice was quiet but she didn't open her eyes, barely moved at all.

She'd always been able to do that, go impossibly still. It was why she was one of the best snipers he'd ever known. The outside world could be going to hell and she'd still be under control. That was his girl: cool, calm, and collected, right up until she put a bullet between your eyes.

She hadn't been raised like most kids though. He understood that. Mainly because his father had been a Marine just like him. He hadn't believed in tears or emotions, just cold, hard logic when tackling a problem. If his dad ever met Skye, he wouldn't know what to make of her. He'd probably end up challenging her to a shooting contest.

"Because you wouldn't have left me like that," he answered.

"You're so sure of that." Her words were cold, flat, stealing the breath from his chest. For a moment only.

But he knew her. In a way she'd never let anyone else see her, and so he knew that she was only trying to protect herself now. That crap wouldn't work on him. "I am sure."

She was silent then, and he let it drop. For now. Only once they were at the safe house would he get his answers. One way or another.

* * *

"Not bad as far as safe houses go. This an Agency one?" Skye asked as they stepped into the two-bedroom condo. The city of Saltillo was industrial yet charming. Most tourists flocked to the west coast of Mexico or to the beaches, completely ignoring parts of the northeastern territory. Which made sense, considering how rampant cartel violence in the state of Coahuila was. Only Saltillo and two other places in

Coahuila were considered safe—that still being a very, very relative word. Hell, US government personnel were only allowed to travel to Saltillo during daylight hours. And forget about traveling to the majority of the rest of the state ever.

"No."

When it was clear he wasn't going to expand any, she did a quick sweep of the sparse place. Sturdy furniture, including two soft beds, no bugs—neither the creepy crawly kind nor listening devices—and running water. Pretty much all she needed for comfort. "So what's the plan?" she asked, trying to ignore the way he made her feel. It had been like that from the moment they'd met. He was a sexy, infuriating distraction. One she'd hated living without.

Leaning against the frame of one of the windows in the small living room, half turned away from her as he looked at his cell phone, he said, "MG is officially safe with her husband. He's got backup with him as well, so they're going to lie low in Corpus Christi. Brooks is putting everyone up in some five-star place using cash."

Skye nodded. Colt had once told her that Brooks's dad was incredibly wealthy. His family owned some sort of ranching dynasty or something. Something to do with horses and cows—things that also terrified her. Why would anyone get up on a giant animal and try to ride it? Even if horses were gorgeous, you could never tell what those beasts were thinking. Cows were even worse.

"And the plan," Colt said, looking up at her as he shoved his phone into his front pocket, "is you give me some answers right now."

No way. "What about Ramirez? I want to make contact."

"He'll be in town in the morning."

"How do you know that?"

"Got the info from one of the analysts working the Coahuila region. Not only do I know where he's going to be tomorrow, I also have copies of recordings from David's brother talking about staging a coup once his father was dead. Nasty stuff. Combined with the blood vials, we'll have a good chance of getting him to back off Mary Grace."

"I have a pretty decent file on the Ramirez family too, but no recordings. That's gold." And oh, how they could use that to their advantage. David Ramirez would kill Rafael if he heard him talking about trying to take over. It would solidify David's position, eliminating any chance he looked weak.

"Does the Agency know you're here?"

"Other than the analyst, not yet. But I'm going to reach out to the lead agent working the Ramirez cartel. Guy will have no problem letting me contact David Ramirez if it means David kills his brother."

"Are you going to tell anyone about me?"

"No."

She relaxed a little. "I'd prefer to meet with David, but if you won't let me, I'll be your backup."

"Good. You're a better shot than me anyway."

She snorted. Long range she was better, only because she was steadier. But he was incredible too. And he'd always insisted he was the best, which meant he was trying to soften her up. Not that it would take much. Living without him had made her edgy.

Skye glanced over to the window. Being so close to him after all this time was torture, especially since she had to conceal her true feelings for him. While every part of her was dying to wrap around him and never let go, she had to pretend she was indifferent.

Dusk had fallen, and though she could eat, she didn't want to head out anywhere. It wasn't as if anyone had gotten a good look at her when she'd rescued Mary Grace, but she tried to keep a low profile everywhere.

"I'm so pissed at you," he snapped abruptly, not exactly a surprise.

She'd be beyond hurt if he had disappeared from her life the way she had from his, but she couldn't make him a target for that psycho. "Colt—"

He moved like lightning, so fast she hadn't even seen him approaching. His mouth was on hers before she could get another word out, his big body pressed up against hers, moving, moving, until her back slammed against something. A wall.

He shoved his fingers through her hair, holding her head in place as he devoured her, seemingly unable to get enough. *Right back at you*—because she couldn't either. Her nipples tightened and heat flooded between her thighs as he ground his hips against her. Doing this was stupid, would only hurt both of them in the long run, but apparently neither of them cared.

Skye knew she sure as hell didn't. Pretending to be indifferent to him? Even she wasn't that good of an actress. Not around Colt anyway. He stripped her until she was emotionally naked, vulnerable, unable to hide who she truly was to him. The man saw straight through to the core of her.

She ached to feel him inside her, had indulged in multiple fantasies about it while she'd been in hiding. Thinking about him, dreaming about him had been torture because touching herself had never been good enough. She'd always been left wanting more, wanting...him. Always him. Only him.

She hated that she'd been cold to him in the vehicle earlier when he said he knew she wouldn't have left him if she hadn't been in danger, but keeping her walls up was the only sane thing to do. The only right thing to do. Too bad they were crumbling down around her.

He nipped her bottom lip, pressed down hard enough to sting and she moaned, reaching for the hem of her shirt and tearing it off. They were both frantic as they undressed each other. Then, she was naked.

Mostly, anyway. She hadn't managed to get her panties off and when Colt saw them, he started to laugh at the text on the front of her boyshort panties that read *It's not going to lick itself.* Just as suddenly all the muscles in his oh-so-fine body tightened and he slammed a hand against the wall, all humor gone.

"Have you been with anyone since you left?" His expression was completely savage, the muscles in his neck pulling tight.

"No! Have you?" Suddenly she was indignant, even though she'd been the one to leave and he'd thought she was dead. But it had only been six months. If he'd been with someone else...

"No." And he looked even angrier—something she hadn't thought was possible—that she'd asked. "And if you had been, I'm not civilized enough to have been okay with it. You're mine."

A thrill shot through her at his words. Oh yeah, he stripped her right to the core. "There's never been anyone but you." Not literally, but once she'd crossed that line with him, she couldn't have slept with someone else. It would have felt wrong on every level.

She'd never thought she'd give her heart so utterly and completely to someone, but just like with everything else in her life, she didn't fall in love half-assed.

Giving a growl of what sounded like approval, he grasped the edge of the underwear and tugged them downward as he went to his knees. She kicked them away as he grabbed one of her legs and threw it over his shoulder.

And he wasn't gentle either. They'd had rough, gentle and everything in between, and she knew what right now was going to be.

Aaaaaand all thought fled her mind as his mouth connected with her core. He held her open wide, tonguing her as if he was starving and she could hardly stand it. He knew every single inch of her body, had kissed and teased it. Just like he was right now.

Her muscles were pulled taut, slickness coated her and all she could do was stare at his dark head as he stroked and teased her with his tongue. She'd missed this, craved Colt and all his raw intensity. Just like her, he never did anything half-assed either. He wouldn't be satisfied until she was coming and moaning out his name. She sucked in a breath, another moan escaping as he zeroed in on her clit.

It wouldn't be long now. She shoved one hand through his hair and cradled her breast with her other. Rolling her nipple back and forth between her thumb and forefinger, she could barely keep her eyes open as he continued teasing her. She wanted to let her head fall back, to give in to the pleasure, but a part of her she didn't want to admit existed was terrified that if she closed her eyes, he'd disappear. That she'd wake up and discover this had all been a dream. She'd wake up alone in one of her shitty safe houses, aching for him and what might have been.

"Feels..." She couldn't even get the word *good* out, much less *incredible* or *spectacular*. His tongue was magic and wonderful and she wanted to always be doing this with him.

"Come," he growled against her slickness.

Her inner walls clenched around nothing, desperate to be filled by him. She could come without it, her body was certainly begging to, but... "In me first," she rasped out.

He let out a strangled sound and pulled away from her. Her leg fell from his broad shoulder as he moved, but her foot didn't have time to touch the floor before he hoisted her up against the wall. Then he pushed her legs farther apart and thrust inside her, invading and taking everything she had to offer.

"Colt!" The feel of him stretching her was way too much and yet not enough. She wrapped her legs around him, her mouth moving toward his even as his head descended toward her.

Scraping her fingers down his back, she savored the feel of all his strength under her fingertips. She'd missed this so much, wanted to drown in him. Her heart ached as he thrust into her, once, twice, over and over, the wall shaking under the impact of their bodies.

Needing to touch him everywhere, she moved her hands to his front, stroking over his skin, over his chest and shoulders before she wrapped her arms around his back again. She couldn't get enough of him.

When he reached between their bodies and started teasing her clit with his thumb, she couldn't hold off anymore. Didn't want to. They had all night. And if this was the only night they got together, she was going to wring every ounce of pleasure out of it she could. She was greedy when it came to him. Always had been. Even if she'd been afraid to fully let go with him.

She started coming around his cock, vaguely aware he didn't have on a condom but she didn't care because she was still on birth control. He growled something against her mouth as she came, her orgasm slamming through her. The pleasure of her climax spiraled out to all her nerve endings, her fingers and toes, until she was gasping.

Her head fell back against the wall with a thud as she rode it out, the sensations almost too much. He joined her, thrusting harder and faster as he found his own release, his hands now on her hips, holding her so tight she knew he'd leave bruises.

Good. She wanted him to mark her, to remember this night. Not that there was a chance she'd forget it. Eventually he stopped moving and when he pulled out of her it was an acute loss she felt bone deep. He cupped one side of her face so gently it almost brought tears to her eyes. But she hadn't cried since...since she'd left him. She'd allowed herself to rage once, then she'd had to bottle it up to survive, to function.

"I've missed you, Skye," he said in a rough voice.

"I've missed you too." She'd missed him like she would miss oxygen. And she wanted to tell him what was wrong, why she'd faked her death. But if she did he'd be all noble and go up against a threat she couldn't find. The threat was simply too big. She'd weighed all her options and come to the conclusion that there was only one way to keep Colt safe. Not only that, if she confessed what she'd done before faking her death, she would put him in an awful position.

He pressed his forehead to hers and closed his eyes—and she was very aware of the stickiness between her thighs. Not only that, but she was sore in a way she hadn't been in a long time. Deliciously sore.

She wasn't sure how long they stood there that way and she didn't care. Time had very little meaning right now.

"I didn't use a condom," he finally murmured. Opening his eyes, he pulled back, but not by much. Just enough so he could look down at her. But his cock was still at half-mast, pressed tight between them.

"I'm on birth control." She'd never gone off. Old habits died hard. She might be physically strong and trained, but more than most she knew how bad the world could be. And she'd been an agent with the CIA for six years. They required all female agents in the field to be on birth control.

Instead of responding, or even grilling her, as she'd suspected he might try, Colt scooped her up as if she weighed nothing and wordlessly headed to the master bathroom. It wasn't large, but the shower stall was more than accommodating for two people.

As the hot water pulsed over them, soaking them, she wrapped her arms around him and held tight. Closing her eyes, she pretended that this was before six months ago, before her life had gone to shit. Before she'd lost the love of her life.

CHAPTER SEVEN

—Home isn't a place.—

Mary Grace couldn't have calmed down even if she'd wanted to. And she didn't. Her heart raced as she waited for the door of the plane to open. The pilot was working with someone at this hangar, which made sense since they'd flown in under the radar.

None of that mattered. The only thing that did was finally getting to see her husband.

Part of her was terrified that this was a dream, that she was still in that house—that prison—and she'd wake up and have her heart ripped out all over again. But no, this was real. And one of her best friends was still in Mexico, determined to make things right for her and Mercer, make it so they'd be safe after all this insanity.

"Come on, come on," she muttered more to herself even though the pilot had stepped into the cabin. She was beyond grateful that she'd been given this freedom, but the seconds ticked by agonizingly slowly.

When the hatch opened, her heart thundered in her chest, the sound so loud in her ears she couldn't hear anything else as the stairs folded out for her. The pilot said something about the coast being clear for them and that this part of the private airport was secure, but she ignored most of it as she stepped into the sunlight.

It took a few moments for her eyes to adjust, but even then, she knew that one of the three blurs in the distance was her husband. She took off down the stairs, not even conscious of starting to move. By the time she hit the pavement, she was full-out sprinting to the man who'd stolen her heart so very long ago when he'd told her she was the one and only he ever wanted to be with.

They'd been fifteen years old then. She loved him even more now than she had then.

He was racing to her as well, his powerful legs eating up the distance faster than she could ever hope to run. He was still blurry and she realized it was because she was crying. God, the tears wouldn't stop. Her face was wet and her throat was tight.

"Mercer." She sobbed out his name as she jumped into his big arms. Her entire body was shaking as she wrapped her arms and legs around him, holding him as tight as he was her. She probably should have thanked the pilot but she absolutely didn't care about anything other than this moment. This man.

"Mary Grace." Her big, normally easygoing husband was sobbing into her hair and neck as he held her tight, his arms like steel bands around her. Her breasts pressed against his chest and she could feel the beat of his heart, just as wild and out of control as hers. "Not letting you go again."

"Not letting you go either." Her words were garbled through her tears so even though that was what she tried to say, she didn't think the words were very clear.

Not that it mattered. He knew what she meant.

A few moments later two other sets of big arms wrapped around them. Without even seeing them she knew who they were.

"God, you're really alive." Brooks's voice was surprisingly thick. "Missed you, woman."

"You're the best of all of us. You're never leaving again."

Savage sounded pretty damn close to tears as well. Something that should have been an impossibility.

Which just made her sob even harder into Mercer's neck. She couldn't stop, couldn't pull back from him. Now that the floodgates had opened—as she'd known they would—she was afraid she'd never stop crying.

She could have been killed in the mountains of Mexico and her husband never would have known. They'd have never had this second chance—or the chance to have a baby together. Something she'd wanted desperately for years. She wanted to tell him right now but couldn't find the words.

She'd wait until they were in private or at least safer than right here out in the open.

As if he'd read her mind, she felt him stalking back toward the hangar, the others' boots pounding against the pavement right alongside them.

"Getting you to a safe house," he murmured against her hair, his familiar voice soothing.

She couldn't pull back from his neck even though she wanted to. Right now her eyes were squeezed shut as she inhaled that familiar, spicy scent she always associated with Mercer. Her man, her life.

At the sound of a vehicle door opening, she pulled back as he slid them into the back seat of an SUV.

"It's one of my dad's. Under one of his company cards," Brooks said, as if she was worried about that.

She should be more worried about her safety, but now that she was here she trusted Mercer to take care of her. For so many months she'd been keeping it together, not having that breakdown she'd desperately wanted to have. Every day she'd stood at that ledge, right on the precipice of losing her mind. Especially when she discovered she was pregnant. It had been like this giant "fuck you" from the universe, giving them this gift but taking away the joy at the same time.

As they settled in, she had no intention of getting off his lap and it was clear he felt the same way. The guys were in the front, giving them the illusion of privacy.

Finally, *finally*, she swiped at her cheeks and fully looked at her husband. She stroked her fingertips over his brown cheeks, just wanting to touch him. When she fully cupped his cheeks, she sighed. She was home. "I never thought this day would come."

"Me neither." His words were harsh, raspy. "My Mary Grace." His grip tightened a fraction as he closed his eyes and laid his forehead against hers.

"You've lost weight," she murmured.

Opening his eyes, he swallowed hard and just searched her face, staring at her as if he'd never seen her before. Or more accurately, as if he'd never thought he'd see her again.

She blinked back more tears and leaned forward, brushing her lips over his. His entire body trembled under her gentle touch.

"It won't take much longer until we're there," Savage said from the front, his voice seeming overloud in the quiet interior.

Mercer grunted in acknowledgment, but she couldn't even muster that much of a response.

Instead, she kissed him again, losing herself in his touch and taste for a long moment. All she could think was that she was finally home. She and their baby were safe now.

CHAPTER EIGHT

—Normal is overrated.—

Eight months ago

Colt lifted his ice-cold beer, tipped it toward Skye's raised glass of wine. "To our first date."

She frowned at him. "This isn't our first date. Not even close."

"Having sex in random places all over the world isn't dating." Though doing that with Skye was the best part of his day. Since they were both stateside and didn't have any scheduled missions for a couple weeks, he'd wanted to do something different tonight. So he'd taken her to a little Italian restaurant outside DC. It wasn't fancy but the food was authentic and they had privacy. Something both of them valued.

"Sure feels like dating. So what happens on regular people dates? Do we get to do kinky stuff after dinner?" She lowered her voice even though they were sitting in a private booth in the corner of the place and there weren't any patrons close enough to hear. Wearing a simple black dress he'd never seen her in before, she looked incredible. Her auburn hair was down tonight, falling around her shoulders in soft waves. So different than the tight, efficient braid she usually sported. "Wait," she continued, before he could answer. "What about that time we rode ATVs through the jungle in...Costa Rica, I think? That was definitely a date."

91

"It wasn't Costa Rica. It was Colombia. And we were running from men armed with assault rifles."

"We had dinner and sex afterward. Maybe not in that order, but it counts."

He just laughed and reached across the small table, sliding his fingers through hers. "What kind of panties do you have on tonight?" She always surprised him with the most random undergarments.

"None." The grin she gave him was wicked and pure Skye.

Ah, hell. It was definitely too early to get the check since they hadn't even gotten their salads yet. So he shifted slightly in his seat. He knew a lot about her: where she'd grown up—between Virginia and Spain; what her favorite music was—jazz; her likes—custom weapons and fast boats; her dislikes—overeducated assholes at the Agency and, for some reason, farm animals. But a lot of the time she kept things on the superficial. He wanted to go deeper with her, wanted all of Skye. The good and the bad.

From what he'd gathered, he'd gotten closer to her than any man she'd been with before. And there hadn't been many. Skye was picky about who she trusted in her bed and she'd confessed that she'd never been with another spy before. No, she'd gone for the artist types, easy males she called all the shots with. Things had definitely changed because she was his now. And he wasn't letting her go. Even if they did butt heads—because no one person called the shots between the two of them. They were a team, in the field and out.

"Who taught you how to shoot?" He'd wanted to ask her for a while, because the way she shot was incredible. The Agency had training, of course, but she had a gift and something told him she'd learned young. His question was really just a segue into more personal details. He was a spy because he was good at reading people, among other reasons. And for the most part, people didn't get into his line of work if they'd had happy childhoods. That wasn't always the case, but he'd venture to guess ninety-five percent of the time it stood to be true.

"My mom."

That surprised him. "Yeah?"

She nodded, took another sip of her wine. "She grew up on a farm out west and shooting was something she learned young."

"Why'd she teach you?"

"I know what you're doing, Mr. Nosy."

"What am I doing?" he asked, dropping his voice an octave, rubbing his thumb over her palm. He loved seeing her in a relaxed setting, her hair literally down. They were on the go all the time and this was different. And he knew that things could be different between them if she opened up more.

She paused as their server delivered two Caesar salads. Once they were alone again, she slightly narrowed her electric blue eyes at him. "Digging for information. And you're not even subtle. I thought you were supposed to be better at your job."

"You're not a job." Never, ever that.

She gave him a faint smile. "Good answer."

"Come on. I want more than surface stuff, Skye. I love you. I'm not in this for something casual. If I wanted casual I'd head to the nearest bar for an easy lay."

Her eyes narrowed. "Your dick is mine, along with the rest of you."

Aaaand that was as close as she'd ever gotten to telling him she loved him. It drove him batshit crazy she wouldn't say the words. Hell, maybe it was *couldn't*. He knew her upbringing hadn't been conventional, and the way she compartmentalized things was legendary in the Agency.

"Fine, my mom taught me because she thought it would be a valuable 'tool in my arsenal.' Instead of taking fun, family vacations, my parents taught me how to construct bombs using household materials. Even during our time in Spain I was always training. Everything was a life lesson. When we'd go to the market my mom would grill me on little things. Like how many people had on hats or how many people had been carrying brown bags. Whatever. It was always something different."

Jesus, he'd thought his dad was rough.

"And forget about friends. Not real ones anyway—except in college. I made a few girlfriends, but..." She shook her head, took a healthy sip of wine this time. "Damn you, Colt Stuart. After this you better tell me something funny."

"I will." Anything to put a smile back on her face. But he wanted to hear this, wanted to peel back the layers of Skye Arévalo. A woman who had him absolutely obsessed and he didn't care. He didn't want her to stop opening up to him though.

"I actually hadn't planned to follow in their footsteps, but when I was twenty they were killed."

"In the line of duty?"

A barely perceptible nod. "Yeah. They died in Beirut. In a bombing. Their stars are on the wall... Something went wrong and the detonator didn't work. They had to detonate it by hand. One of them could have gotten out, so they must have made the decision to die together. I didn't actually know the facts until I was recruited by the Agency and got the right clearance... You know, you could just look this stuff up about me," she said quietly, watching him carefully. "Not all of it, but you'd be able to piece together things about my parents if you wanted."

He had the right clearance, the same as her. He knew he could have looked this up if he wanted. He didn't. "I want to know what you want me to know. Not go behind your back." She didn't respond for a long moment, just picked at her salad. He did the same, though he didn't remember tasting any of it. "It was good they went together," she finally said. "Neither would have wanted to live without the other."

"I'm sorry."

She lifted a shoulder. "They loved what they did. The ironic thing is, I'd never planned to follow in their footsteps. I was sure trained for it, but looking back I realize they didn't raise me the way they did because they wanted me to be like them. They just wanted to make sure that if something happened to them, I'd be able to take care of myself, to always have situational awareness. They gave me the most incredible gift. Wish I'd realized that sooner."

He cleared his throat as she went back to her salad. "I want to take you home. To Redemption Harbor, I mean." It was the only place he'd likely ever call home. As far as physical places went. Because the truth was, when he was with Skye he felt like he was home in a way he couldn't describe. Didn't need to. He'd been holding off asking her this for a while because he didn't want to spook her. But it was time to bring her home, to meet the people he considered family. Right on the South Carolina coast with a population of about fifty thousand, it was an eclectic artists' paradise. There were beaches, harbors, and heck of a lot of good people.

Her eyebrows raised slightly as she met his gaze. "I feel like I know your friends already. Especially Mary Grace and Mercer. Jeez, those two are hilarious. I can't believe he ended up opening a pizza joint after playing pro ball."

"If you'd ever seen him eat a pizza, you would. He acts like a freaking Ninja Turtle where pizza is concerned." And it was more than one pizza joint; he'd opened a few because the man had a head for business.

She barked out an unexpected laugh. "A Ninja Turtle? I swear you're a twelve-year-old half the time," she murmured, pausing only when their server came by to pick up their barely eaten salads to replace them with the entrees.

"Did I ever tell you how Mercer almost turned his back on going pro?" His friend had almost quit during his senior year of college. He'd been heavily scouted too.

"Uh uh." She took a sip of her wine, glancing over the rim of the glass at him with curiosity. "What happened?"

"He came forward about some teammates involved in a rape scandal. Testified against them."

"Damn."

"Yeah, no shit. He lost a lot of so-called friends, but he told me once he never regretted his decision. Not that I would have expected a man like him to."

"You respect him."

"Hell, yeah. He sees the world in black and white, right and wrong. For him, there's not often a gray area. I might not always agree, but respect? Yep."

"Well I know he got picked up anyway, so it obviously didn't hurt his career."

Colt snorted. "The opposite. He got two endorsements his first year. Everyone wanted him as their poster boy. It was a pretty safe bet he wasn't going to cause labels any embarrassment."

"So why'd he retire so early? I don't know much about sports, but from what it sounds like he's still in his prime. He's in his early thirties, right?"

"Yeah, thirty-four. But he got burned out, no more love for it—I'm just guessing, because he's never flat out said why. I also think he wanted to move home with his wife, be out of the spotlight so they could start a family and live normal lives. He was never into the 'baller' lifestyle. For him it was love of the game and a way to make a lot of money. He majored in business."

"This is the best damn Italian I've ever had," Skye said after a few moments of eating her eggplant parmigiana. "You were right about this place."

"I'm always right." He grinned when she rolled her eyes. "You know, when we first met I thought you were working an angle." Her bold, unexpected admission took him off guard. "I kept waiting for the other shoe to drop. Then I found out...that after our first few missions you requested to keep working with me. I thought maybe you were in charge of an internal investigation and that was the reason for the request. But after some digging I realized nope, you just wanted to work with me."

"We're a good team." And he'd fallen head over heels for her. He hadn't wanted another partner, not after seeing how they were together. Sometimes it was as if she read his mind, knew what he was going to do before he'd made the decision. That was important to have in a partner.

She nodded, spearing a piece of her food with her fork. "Yeah, we are."

Then why won't you say you love me? "So when did you officially decide I wasn't investigating you?"

"The first night we got naked together."

He grinned and took a bite of his carbonara. That sounded about right. Skye would never let anyone into her bed who she didn't trust. Or in their case, it had been up against a wall that first time. Then in the shower. He couldn't even remember when they'd finally made it to an actual bed.

The only thing he knew for sure about Skye was that he wasn't letting her go. He just wished she would trust him enough to let all her walls down, to fully give him her heart. Because she certainly trusted him to have her back on missions. But something had to give. He wanted all of her.

CHAPTER NINE

—I'll always have your six.—

Mary Grace sat on Mercer's lap, feeling safe for the first time in months. The drive to this "safe house"—aka a luxury hotel—was a blur. All she'd been focused on was her husband, on the way he'd quietly held her.

Now she curled up against him, glad he was so big. Her sexy husband was rock-hard despite his obsession with pizza. She wrapped an arm around his massive shoulders, resting her hand lightly on the opposite one. Being with him was being home, even if they weren't in their actual home.

Unfortunately, two of their best friends, Brooks and Savage, refused to leave them alone even though they were safe now. Well, unfortunately was the wrong word, because she was so incredibly grateful to have such good friends in her life. Friends who had watched out for her husband when they'd thought she was dead. Her heart ached at all those months he'd gone through without her, thinking the worst. She swallowed back the lump in her throat, not wanting to have another breakdown. She'd already cried her eyes out; she'd save the rest of her tears for when they were finally back in Redemption Harbor.

"What are you holding back?" Savage asked quietly, the question breaking through the light conversation they'd been having.

It was as if everyone wanted to avoid talking about her being gone, or about the Ramirez cartel. Instead they'd been talking about silly stories from high school or holidays. She wanted to focus on reality.

"What the hell are you talking about? My wife just got back from a living hell." Mercer's entire body tightened under her, her husband looking as if he wanted to jump up and pummel Savage.

She kept her arms wrapped around his shoulders and snuggled closer. "No, his question is fair. I appreciate the attempt to not upset me, but Colt risked his life for me. So did the woman with him. I'm not exactly holding back...but Colt knows the woman who rescued me and he's in love with her. As in, completely and utterly in love with her. I don't know her name, but since he works for the CIA, and based on some of their vague and frightening conversations—and her training—it's clear she works for them, or did. She faked her death for some reason." Mary Grace felt a little bad telling the others, but no one in this suite would tell anyone outside it. They'd all been friends forever and she wasn't so sure that Colt didn't need backup. No matter what he said. "I'm worried about them, even if they are trained. I feel like they're walking into a lion's den."

Savage let out a colorful curse, making everyone look at him.

"What?" Brooks asked, the first thing he'd said in a while. Like usual, he had on a worn cowboy hat and boots and would fit in right where they were. You'd never know the guy was a freaking billionaire, thanks to his family legacy.

"I have an idea who the woman is," Savage muttered. "It's just a guess. About six months ago Colt went completely dark for about a month after his new partner died."

Everyone nodded because Mary Grace remembered that as well. Not the partner dying part—she'd only been guessing about Colt's career—but she remembered not being able to get ahold of him for weeks. But it had been before her big trip to Mexico and eventually he'd called her back so she'd let the radio silence go. Now she wished she'd pushed because he'd seemed a little off in the last couple months before she'd left. They'd only talked on the phone a few times since he was always gone, but he'd been different. Almost subdued.

Savage continued. "You don't have the security clearance for this information, but screw it. I'm going to tell you who I think it might be. Does she have red hair and an olive complexion? She's fluent in a few languages as well."

Mary Grace nodded. "Yes, she stunning. And maybe a little crazy."

Savage grinned at that. "Yeah, that sounds about right. Her name is Skye. And she is listed as dead. I always wondered about that because she seemed invincible."

"You know her how?" Mercer asked.

"I was attached to a couple jobs she did overseas. Before she teamed up with Colt, I believe. The Agency hired me for some contract stuff. I heard some rumors they'd gotten together but he never said anything."

Well that wasn't vague or anything, but Mary Grace didn't push. Now wasn't the time. "Well obviously she's in trouble if she faked her own death. And the woman risked her neck for me simply because Colt knew and cared about me."

"Do you know where he's going exactly?" Mercer asked, looking at Brooks.

"No, and he's gone dark again. Once he knew MG was here with us, he said he'd contact me 'when MG is safe from the cartel,' then hung up on me. I've tried calling him back and texting. No response. He might have ditched the phone."

Savage cursed again, which was standard for the guy.

Sighing, Mary Grace looked up at her husband. She'd wanted to wait until they were alone but clearly that was never going to happen. And she wanted her friends to know too. Since there wasn't much—anything—they could do for Colt or the woman whose name was apparently Skye, it was time to tell Mercer about the baby. "I've got something else to tell you."

Mercer tensed, watching her with midnight eyes she'd been looking into with love and lust since she was fifteen.

"You're going to be a father. I'm about three months along."

His mouth opened once, then shut. At her news, Savage and Brooks murmured under their breaths about checking on something in the next room. Then she and Mercer were alone, though she could hear the two uncles-to-be in the kitchenette, likely eavesdropping.

Mercer shifted slightly and moved his big, callused hands to her covered belly as joy infused his expression. "I thought I felt a little bump, but I thought..." Awe tinged his voice.

She giggled. "You thought I'd gained weight."

"I don't care if you gain fifty pounds," he murmured, oh so gently brushing his lips over hers as if he was afraid to hurt her. "What do you need? Are you okay? Should you be sitting in a certain position? I know you're a doctor, but should I call someone? What—"

"Mercer!" She took his face in her hands, stroked her thumbs over the dark brown skin of his cheeks—which apparently Brooks had made him shave before coming to the airport.

They'd been trying for a year to get pregnant before her trip with no luck so this was more than welcome news. But she had a feeling he was going to be a tad overprotective from this point forward.

"I'm okay. I'll need to get on prenatal vitamins but I've been eating healthy and I wasn't hurt by anyone there." She'd been stressed out too, and okay, she was nervous and would be until she had an ultrasound and met with her doctor, but she wasn't going to tell him that. Right now she just wanted to keep the joy on her husband's face.

"I love you so much, Mary Grace. When I thought you were gone, I thought...our dreams of a family were gone forever." His voice cracked as he pulled her into the gentlest hug ever, his big body vibrating with emotions.

Laying her head on his shoulder, she hugged him right back, safe and secure in the arms of the most noble, honest man she'd ever known. And she thanked God that they'd been given this second chance.

Now they just needed to get their friend—and his mystery woman—back to safety.

* * *

Colt watched as Skye stepped out of the condo's bathroom into the small master bedroom. Instead of going the wig route, she'd died her hair brunette with a temporary color, added clip-in bangs of the same color and pulled her hair back into a twist at the back of her neck. Instead of pale blue eyes, she looked at him with chocolate brown ones courtesy of contacts.

With the changes and her skin color, she'd blend in much better now. She'd also added something to the top of her ears to subtly alter the shape for any potential facial recognition software. While the software helped intelligence agencies, it wasn't difficult to fool it if you knew what you were doing.

The hair and eyes weren't for the software, but the ear change was and...her cheeks were slightly different too. She must have rolled-up gauze in them. Or something. "I'm almost done," she said, reaching into her backpack and pulling out a fake pair of glasses. Something that would also interfere with any software.

If for some reason someone who knew her spotted her on the street, it was possible they'd recognize her, but the software wouldn't ping her and associate her face with her name. Which was the whole point.

He took a step toward her, needing to have an actual conversation with her this morning. They'd had a lot of sex last night—and some early this morning. But she'd started pulling away from him again. And not in the typical "get ready for a mission" type of focus. She was shutting him out. Unacceptable. "After this job—"

"Colt, I can't."

"Can't what?"

"Can't get my life back, can't..." Clearing her throat, she zipped up the weathered backpack and slipped it on. Her sniper rifle was inside it—disassembled.

"Whatever you're running from, let me help you." He planned to regardless, but he didn't want to have to fight her over it.

"Let's just make sure Mary Grace is safe. One step at a time."

He knew she was deflecting, trying to blow him off. After the night they'd shared he'd thought she'd be ready to open up to him, but he should have known better. When Skye made up her mind about something, she turned being stubborn into an art form. "Fine. You ready?"

Faint surprise lit her now dark eyes, likely because he wasn't arguing with her. She picked up a brown newsboy cap and put it on. "Let's do this."

According to the agent running the division that focused on the Coahuila region, David Ramirez was meeting with one of his government contacts in an hour. Which would give Colt and Skye enough time to set up an impromptu meeting with him.

They'd have no backup if things went south, but it was a risk he was willing to take. He hated that Skye was taking any risk, but this was the life she'd chosen and he loved her strength, her sense of duty. She had no reason to be here with him, but she had insisted. That was just who she was.

He'd already scanned the feeds of the covert cameras he'd set up outside the condo and there hadn't been any unusual activity. Once outside in the fresh, dry air, he and Skye both scanned the street. The weather was temperate, in the low seventies with no humidity so more people would be out today.

She gave him a quick nod and though he wanted to reach out and kiss her, show any sort of affection, he simply nodded back and headed west while she headed east. Even if he hated leaving her, hated having her out of his sight because not so deep down he was terrified he'd never see her again, they had to do this. He knew she'd have his back; that wasn't the problem. It was what would happen after they'd ensured that Mary Grace was safe.

He was terrified that Skye planned to walk away from him again. Now that he knew she was alive, he'd never stop hunting until he found her. But holy hell, he didn't want to go through that.

He'd be confronting David Ramirez directly in the *Plaza de Armas* by the fountain with the bronze nymphs. At least that was the plan. The walk was quick and uneventful. People were on their way to work, others on their way to one of the universities and yet others just out to enjoy the day. There was a reason Saltillo was referred to as *La Ciudad del Clima Ideal*—the city of perfect climate. Once he reached the colonial city center, built in the unique pink marble it was known for, he took his time, scanning the people even though he wasn't expecting a threat. Not yet, and not at all if he did this right.

Keeping his gait even as he strolled along, he stopped at a local shop to buy a *café de olla* before making his way to one of the wrought iron benches facing the bronze and stone fountain in the middle of the public square. Smiling politely at a college-aged woman who gave him a long, lingering look as she walked by, he pulled out one of his burner phones and texted his CIA contact. Almost immediately he received a response letting him know that Ramirez had left his meeting and was on foot. Next Colt dialed the only number saved inside this phone.

David Ramirez's annoyed voice came through the line after three rings. *"¿Quién es este?"*

This was one of Ramirez's private numbers, not easily accessible to anyone other than his family. Instead of speaking in Spanish, Colt opted for English, not bothering to disguise his voice. He was going to be mostly honest about who he was. "Mr. Ramirez, I'd like to talk to you about what happened two days ago at your family compound."

There was a short pause, then, "Who the fuck is this?" he asked in perfect English, almost no hint of an accent.

"My name isn't important, but I have something you want. I work for the CIA." There had been a few times in his career he'd been honest about who he worked for because it served his purpose. Now was one of them. "We have a mutual interest in that we'd like you to stay in power. Your brother will make a move to take over soon. He also killed your father, not that doctor." Colt let the words sink in.

"You don't know what you're talking about."

"Yes, I do. And you know there's truth in my words or you wouldn't still be on the line. I'm sitting in the middle of the *Plaza de Armas*. I'm alone but not without backup. Bring your men or don't. But if you want the proof that your brother killed your father, among other things I believe you'll find very interesting, meet me here in ten minutes. I'm sitting on a bench in the center."

"I'm too far away—"

"I see our relationship is already off to a bad start, since you're lying to me. You're five minutes away since you just left your meeting with that weak government official, Garcia. Be here in ten. I'm giving you five to make a decision. If you attempt to kill me, the same woman who destroyed half your compound will finish the job—and you." Colt ended the call, not bothering to tell him what he looked like. Ramirez would figure it out. Next he slid a Bluetooth in his ear and called Skye on one of her burners.

She answered immediately. "I've got you in my line of sight. You think he'll show?"

He loved knowing she was watching over him through her scope right now. "He'll either show or have me followed and try to kidnap me once I'm somewhere alone—or kill me." That was the thing about being a spy. Sometimes you had to take balls-to-the-wall risks. Right now he could only hope that Ramirez didn't try to off him before they spoke. That was on the outside realm of possibilities, but Colt liked to be prepared for any scenario. It was why he was armed and had Skye as his backup. Not the best scenario—definitely not as good as having a full tactical team as backup—but if Ramirez or his men made a move she'd start taking his guys out. And she was damn fast; could eliminate at least three guards in seconds. It would give Colt a chance to take cover, then return fire.

"He might try. I'll take him out." There was an edge to her voice that was so familiar it made him ache inside.

He'd missed her, missed working with her, missed the light she brought to his life. It didn't matter that he knew she was alive—a part of him hadn't come to terms with her being in his life again. His brain hadn't caught up to the new reality and that wasn't like him. He adjusted, adapted. Always had. Colt shook it off though. He was about to go toe to toe with a ruthless man. He needed his head fully in this, no outside distractions.

As a woman approached, a little dog on a leash in front of her, she made a move as if to sit next to him.

"*Asiento tomado,*" he said abruptly. He kept his expression hostile, which made her hurry away—but not before giving him an obscene hand gesture. He nearly laughed. Good for her.

"Aw, you hurt her feelings," Skye said into his earpiece. "Look alive, Ramirez is entering from the west. Two guys with him that I can see. They're fanning out on either side as he heads to the center."

"You have titanium balls, Mr. CIA," Ramirez said, sitting on the bench next to him, his moves economic and elegant. Wearing a three-piece Brioni suit in a dark shade of blue—no doubt custom fit—he gave a pleasant smile. Nothing about him seemed agitated. His toothpaste-commercial smile was easy, his dark hair short, with every strand in place. His father had spent his money well, teaching David to appear polished and civilized. Too bad under all that sleek veneer was just another greedy criminal who made his money on the pain of others. But he was the lesser of two evils and in Colt's world, shades of gray ruled. Nothing was ever simple.

Colt lifted a shoulder. "What I have is information you need. I have multiple recordings of your brother and his associates planning to kill you and take over. He thinks you're weak." Colt glanced around, spotted one of Ramirez's men watching from two benches down, hand resting on his hip and the holster there. Not even trying to be subtle.

"How do I know what you have is legitimate?"

Colt slid a hand into his pocket and paused when Ramirez made a move as if to go for a weapon. "I'm pulling out a flash drive."

He nodded once, then made a slight hand motion to his guys to stay put.

"You can easily have this tested for authenticity, but I don't think you need to. You know the truth about Rafael." Colt didn't say out loud that his brother was a psycho because it was one thing for everyone to know it, but it was another to insult the man's family to his face. "He had some interesting things to say about your wife as well on there."

After a short pause, Ramirez took what Colt held out. "So say this proves my brother is trying to stage a coup. This has nothing to do with the doctor. She must pay for her crime."

Colt looked off into the distance, watching as people went about their everyday lives. For the most part, in every city, in every country of the world, people were the same. The majority of them were just trying to get by, trying to live their lives in peace. They wouldn't have any idea what was transpiring on this bench right in front of them. "I also have vials of your father's blood that she took before the escape. Your father was poisoned, something you might already know if you've had it tested yourself. The doctor had no reason to kill him. In fact killing him would have been exponentially stupid, and she is a brilliant woman. You have to know that, unless you're stupid—and we both know that you're not."

Ramirez gave him a long, hard look. "My father was very close to death. Killing him would not have made sense. But he died the same night the trained woman attacked my family's compound."

"The doctor didn't kill your father. She took the Hippocratic Oath, which might mean nothing to some doctors. But she was under your roof for months. You really think she's a killer?"

Ramirez didn't respond. Which was a no.

"When someone came to rescue her, she took the chance. The timing just happened to be...strange. You could blame the murder and subsequent rescue on your brother. It wouldn't be hard to believe that he orchestrated the rescue and the murder of your father in an attempt to set her up, knowing that he'd be able to go after her later and finish the job. If you kill him, no one would question your strength." So if Ramirez was worried about saving face by letting the doctor go, this was the way to do it. Kill the guilty party. His own brother. No one would question that. "What do you say? Is the doctor free from you?"

"If this recording checks out...she'll mean nothing to me, to my organization. No one will bother her."

"You don't need the vials of blood?"

He shook his head. So he'd already tested his father's blood. And he had to know that his brother was behind it. Once David Ramirez heard what his brother had to say about wanting to rape his wife, among other nasty things, Colt had a feeling David would do more than simply put a bullet in Rafael's head.

He'd make an example of him and make people fear him even more. "The flash drive will check out."

Ramirez lifted his shoulder once. "Then she's free."

Colt looked him full in the eyes then. "If she dies, the CIA will come after you. They'll wipe you and your entire compound off the face of the earth with a JDAM, just like they did with Gonzalez—and his entire family and crew. They'll just let another asshole take over the region."

Ramirez lifted a dark eyebrow. "You care about this doctor?"

He snorted. "You don't get to kidnap one of our citizens with no repercussions. We've already set up a recording from her detailing her time in captivity with your cartel. If she dies, we'll send it to all the news agencies anonymously. For now she's not going to tell anyone who kidnapped her. We're going to keep everything quiet and spin a story about her bravery and survival after a town was massacred. The town *your* brother took out. If she dies you can believe there will be a public uproar. An innocent doctor who gives of her skills and time freely in Third World countries is murdered by vicious cartel leader who has an American education—and a very beautiful American wife. The headlines write themselves. And the US government will have no choice but to retaliate because of the media shitstorm. Even narcos aren't above media scrutiny. Not one like you, anyway. You have too many ties to the US." Most of what he said was bullshit. At least at the moment. Because Colt *was* going to have Mary Grace make a recording and he was going to use that as insurance. And he would personally go after Ramirez if he ever tried to hurt her again.

Ramirez paused for a long moment, looking thoughtful. "The woman who rescued the doctor, she is with you?"

"She currently has your head in the sight of her rifle scope."
Sometimes you had to remind the monster who was in charge.

Ramirez stilled, his eyes going glacial.

"I told you I had backup. And before you go," Colt continued. "I want you to understand something. If you go back on your word, they'll take everything from you that matters." Then he started reciting the addresses of the private schools Ramirez's kids went to. It was beyond wrong, but sometimes when dealing with the monsters of the world you had to take on the role of one. Colt would never hurt children, but he needed to drive the point home. Because Ramirez was the kind of man who *would* go after an entire family if it was in his best interest.

Ramirez went completely immobile, red creeping up his neck as his eyes went molten with rage. "If you touch—"

"I'm not doing anything. I'm a simple messenger. I just wanted to make sure we were on the same page. No matter how insulated you think you are down here in Mexico, there's always someone who can take away the people you care about. Take your life away. Always." Standing, Colt straightened his shirt then strode away.

"One of his guys is tailing you... Nope, two," Skye said as he rounded the fountain.

"I figured." No way Ramirez would target him here though.

"What do you think?" she asked.

"I think he's going to have his hands full taking over for his father, and going after one civilian will be a waste of his time and resources. Especially when he'll be able to make an example of his brother and establish himself as a ruthless leader."

"We should still make sure Mary Grace lies low for a few weeks, just to be safe."

He liked the use of "we" but tried not to read into it. Skye was impossible to read and he still didn't have a clue about her intentions after this. "I'm going to catch one of the trollies. I'll meet you at our rendezvous point." A place far outside town. He'd be able to lose a tail in the city, but the place they were supposed to meet at was rural enough that they'd notice anyone following them. He preferred to use main roads since the back ones were rife with narcos, but right now that wasn't an option.

And in reality, he was more worried that Skye would bail on him and not meet at the rally point than concerned about Ramirez targeting him. They'd done what she set out to do and it would be damn easy for her to disappear again. She'd done it once and she had to know he'd never reveal the truth to the Agency.

He'd never betray her. Not for anything. Not even to keep her.

CHAPTER TEN

—Some people just need a high five. In the head.
With a golf club.—

With his feet kicked up on his lounge chair, the man now known as Terrence Pace stared at the report he'd just been sent from one of his many contacts around the world. Waves from the Pacific crashed in the distance, his California villa offering him the amount of privacy he enjoyed.

Frowning, he scanned the pertinent facts. The Ramirez cartel had been attacked two nights ago and it wasn't by another cartel they were warring with.

Not that he particularly cared about any of the cartels, but he liked to keep an eye on any power players that might affect him. Even those who might not. Because the world was set up on dominoes and there had to be a certain structure. Even among cartels. Some kept regions more stable than others. The reason this report had his interest was because of the specific doctor who'd been thought dead but had been rescued, the amount of destruction, and the rumors that *one* person had been behind it all.

A woman.

The woman part wasn't all that surprising. Women were just as vicious and conniving as men. And they could often get into places men couldn't because of their pretty faces. It was why intelligence agencies all around the world utilized their expertise, and had since long before any women's rights movements.

It was the amount of destruction, the use of C4 combined with the strategic setup that caught his eye. And the fact that all the stops had been pulled out to rescue this doctor. Whoever it was, someone had rescued Mary Grace Jackson—a doctor who at one time had been a potential target for him. And no one was taking responsibility for it. Hell, it hadn't even hit the media. He only knew because he kept his ear to the ground. The doctor's family hadn't hired a kidnap negotiator—because everyone had assumed she was dead. Or he hadn't been able to find any information that the husband had hired someone.

It was also strange that this rescue hadn't hit the media. At all. The CIA and a few other US government agencies knew about it, that much he was certain. Yet no one knew—or no one was admitting they knew—who'd rescued the woman. Since this woman had been of semi-importance to an agenda he'd had at one time, he needed to look into this.

Especially since the type of skill set it would have taken to rescue someone the way this mystery woman had…That took serious training. He knew a handful of agents—male and female—who could pull that off.

One in particular who could have done it blindfolded. But she was dead. Or she'd led the world to believe she was. If Skye Arévalo had faked her death she'd done a damn good job of it. Because even he'd believed it. He'd been watching when she'd walked into that warehouse, when it had exploded into a ball of orangey flames.

Setting the report on the glass table next to him, he pulled one of his many cell phones out. "Get in touch with Rafael Ramirez," he said when his contact, a go-between for criminals, answered. "I have some questions for him. Tell him I'm a weapons dealer. Pick one of my aliases. I don't care what you have to say to set up a meeting."

"Right away, sir."

He ended the call, his gaze straying over the expansive lawn of the home owned by his alias, Terrence Pace. He had retirement accounts, and on paper appeared like a legitimate businessman. And that was the way he liked it. He also had more aliases just like this. Some were nothing more than paper with no property attached to them. He even had retirement accounts under his real name as well, with a pension that was much too small for the kind of life he deserved. All in all, Pace was one of his favorite aliases. And Rafael Ramirez would be a better choice to meet with than his brother now that David Ramirez had taken over the cartel.

Rafael was weak and psychotic on the best of days. Luckily it would be easy to stroke his ego and pull information from him. The fool wouldn't even know he was digging for info.

He doubted that Skye was still alive, but the details and the identity of the rescued doctor bothered him. And he'd learned never to ignore his instincts. If Skye was somehow behind this, he'd make her pay for betraying him.

She'd stolen for him, and he'd been so close to getting what he wanted, to retire with millions upon millions. Too much to ever spend. He'd been siphoning off money from various places over the years, stockpiling weapons and untraceable funds—namely jewels—even when he'd been with the Agency. But stealing and then selling that bioweapon would have been his big score. *The biggest.* Because he'd had the perfect buyer lined up.

Then she'd died, taking his retirement plan with her. Since her death he'd been working toward finding someone else to steal what he needed. Unfortunately the only company who had what he wanted had increased their security a hundred-fold.

So if he found out she was alive, that she'd wasted his time, his resources... He'd kill everyone she loved before he was finished with her. He'd make her watch, suffer until she was ready for death.

CHAPTER ELEVEN

—When life is tough, put on your boxing gloves.—

"This definitely isn't one of the worst places I've stayed in." Skye scanned the pay-by-the-hour motel, a half-smile on her gorgeous face.

"Definitely not the worst," Colt agreed. They'd slept in tents, out in the jungle, and occasionally the desert. Overall he preferred the mountains if he had to sleep out in the open. "Glad to be on American soil." Even if they'd only been just across the border. There was a certain feeling he got when he was on his home turf.

Skye shrugged noncommittally and he knew it was because for her, whatever threat she was running from didn't end at a border.

Yeah, he was going to come back to that, but first he pulled out one of his burners and called Mercer. "You guys good?" he asked his buddy the second he picked up.

"Yeah. Hell, yeah. You're going to be an uncle."

Colt smiled at the pride he could hear in his friend's voice. To think they'd almost lost Mary Grace. "I know."

"And you better tell *Skye* I'm meeting her in person."

Colt glanced at Skye, who was peeking out the plain beige curtain hanging in front of the window. It only had a few stains on one of the panels. Looked like coffee. Despite the mid-seventy degree weather of Corpus Christi, air was blowing out of the window air conditioner box, making the curtain ripple.

"Okay." He didn't want to ask how Mercer knew her name, for multiple reasons. Colt had been careful about not using her name, so Mary Grace hadn't known it. And since Skye was clearly running from something, he didn't want to talk about this over the phone, even if these were secure. Because the truth was, nothing was truly secure. Not unless you met in a SCIF—a Sensitive Compartmented Information Facility.

"Savage thinks he knows who she is."

"Ah." Well that was interesting, and Colt wasn't sure he liked that at all.

"So what's the deal? We're still in Texas. Where are you? Are you finally safe?"

"We are."

"You in the same city as us?"

He really didn't want to lie to his friend. But if he told him yes, Mercer would want them to meet with them. And Colt needed time with Skye alone first. "We're close."

"Fine, be vague... I'm hoping you have good news for us?"

"I think MG's safe, but we won't know for a few weeks. I'll tell you all the details in person, but I think it should be okay to return home. Just...don't stay in your house. In case Ramirez goes back on his word."

Mercer let out a sigh of relief. "All right. You know where we'll be, then."

He did. Brooks had a few extra homes on his family's massive spread of property, usually for the hands, who found it easier to live and work on site during cattle breeding season. But knowing Brooks, he'd have their friends staying right in the main house. He'd want them close, to be able to watch out for them.

"And I've got people running the restaurants. Not that I care. They've been doing it for the last couple months anyway. The only thing that matters is I've got my girl with me. And I'm not letting her out of my sight again. Thank you, Colt. For what you did. I... Hell, you get free pizza for life."

He snorted at Mercer's words. "I get free pizza already."

"Maybe I'll name my kid after you."

"Not if it's a girl!" Mary Grace's voice was clear enough in the background that Colt figured she was probably sitting in Mercer's lap.

"Yeah, if it's a girl we're naming her Skye," Mercer said. "So when are you headed home?"

"I...don't know." He needed to figure out some things with Skye, then come up with a plan of attack for how they were going to face down whatever threat she was up against.

"Since you've given us the go-ahead, we're all headed out tomorrow on the plane." Meaning Brooks's plane. "Come with us. Bring your girl too. It's clear she's dealing with some serious stuff from what Mary Grace told us. Let's help her."

"Mercer—"

"Don't 'Mercer' me! We're your friends. Hell, we're your family. Now the woman who saved my wife's life is family too—a woman you apparently love. Gage said he'd meet us at home as soon as we got there. He wanted to come here but I told him to hold off. And I've left a message with Leighton. Once I hear back, you know he'll head home too. No more lone ranger bullshit, Colt. Come home."

"I wouldn't argue with him," Mary Grace said in the background.

He'd always wanted to take Skye to his home, but never had the chance. "All right. We'll be there. What airport are you flying out of?" Out of the corner of his eye, he saw Skye straighten and look at him, but he ignored her. If he had to hogtie her, they'd both be there.

After giving Colt the name, Mercer said, "We're planning to leave at ten. But we'll wait for you."

"Okay. I'll call you in the morning. Watch your six."

"You too."

"Where are 'we' going to be?" Skye asked warily, stepping away from the window. She gave the flowered bedspread a dubious look, then sat at the small table close to the door instead.

"We're headed back to Redemption Harbor tomorrow with my friends. And save it." He shook his head, moving closer so that he was in between her and the door. "You're coming even if I have to physically restrain you."

Her gaze narrowed, but she didn't shift from her seat. Just sighed, looking more exhausted than he'd ever seen her. "God, you're so pigheaded. Can't you just leave well enough alone?" she shouted at him, her jaw clenched tight.

"How about no? The woman I love—"

She jumped to her feet and then shoved him in the chest. "Shut the hell up with that love bullshit! I lied to you, I disappeared, you mourned because of me. You can't love me. It makes no sense!"

"Wrong. I do."

Her cheeks flushed even redder—purely from rage—as she faced off with him. "What the hell is the matter with you? I'm an asshole. You can't love me."

"I *know* you're an asshole. And I still love you. Maybe I love you because of your asshole-ness." He poked her once in the chest, knowing it would make her crazy, and hopefully bring her even closer to finally telling him what the hell was going on.

"There's something wrong with you," she snapped. "I've given you every reason to hate me. To just walk away and abandon me."

Lifting his shoulders casually—and watching as the action pissed her off even more—he smiled. "Yet I don't, and I won't. Sounds like you're the one with the problem. Maybe it's because you think you're unlovable?"

"Shut. Up."

"No. I knew you loved me long before you could admit it. And that's on you. You think you're unlovable for some reason I'll never understand. Good thing for the both of us I've got more than enough love for you."

She practically flinched at the L word, always had. Then, instead of the wall he'd gotten used to with her, all her anger broke through. It was almost as if he could watch the wall crumbling around her, she was so pissed. "You are such...an annoying—"

"Loveable."

"Frustrating—"

"Loveable."

"Jackass of epic proportions! I want to throat punch you so bad right now." Her hands balled into fists at her sides.

He tilted his head slightly to the side, surprised steam wasn't coming out of her ears as he watched her. "I think you mean you want to fuck me," he murmured.

"Argh!" She pulled a fist back and he moved fast, kicking the flimsy chair out of the way as he shoved her up against the wall, pinning her in place with his body.

"I'll fuck you right here, right now, and you'll love every second of it. But it'll let you ignore what's between us, let you ignore what you've been running from. So that's not happening. If you want to go toe to toe with me, both of us will get hurt, but I guaran-fucking-tee that I will have you on that plane tomorrow. So get over your bullshit and tell me what you're running from."

To his surprise, and okay, *horror*, tears formed in her eyes and she buried her face against his chest. For a second, because he knew Skye's training, he thought this might be a ploy, but her entire body shook as she wrapped her arms around him and cried.

Simply cried, something he'd never seen her do. Even when she'd broken a finger in the jungle once, she'd blinked back any tears that might dare to fall. As if the tears offended her.

It felt like his chest was caving in.

Rubbing his hand up and down her spine, he let her cry and held her close. He hated her tears, but he was glad she was letting go. Finally. Because whatever, or whoever, she was running from had to be bad. And he was going to *destroy* whoever had brought her to this state.

He wasn't sure how long she cried, and didn't care. She eventually pulled back and, sniffing once, swiped at her cheeks.

Her eyes were still glassy, the blue even brighter than normal, her eyelids puffy. "Your shirt's all messed up," she muttered.

"Like I care."

Her lips pulled up into a half-smile. "I don't know why I said that. So, let's talk…I guess."

"Yeah, let's talk." He pulled out the chair for her, then pulled the other one around and sat in front of her, blocking her exit.

She gave an exhausted sigh. "I'm not going to run."

"I just like being close to you. You smell good and I—"

"Don't say you love me." She gave a pathetic attempt at a snarl, but it fell short. When he didn't respond, she continued.

"I'm just going to start at the beginning. You're definitely going to get pissed, so just keep all of it to yourself, as well as any questions, until I'm done. Okay?"

He nodded. "Okay."

She took a deep breath and he took her hands in his. She startled a little, but linked her fingers through his. "About a month before I disappeared, I was contacted by someone."

"Who?" he demanded.

She pursed her lips.

"Sorry."

"I was contacted by a man. He wanted me to steal a bioweapon. A new strain of screwed-up shit that humans invented," she muttered, shaking her head in disgust. "I know you don't need the details. Anyway, he had me backed into a corner. I had to do what he wanted." When it looked as if he might interrupt, Skye shook her head. "Let me finish. I stole the weapon from HMX."

Colt nodded, clearly understanding why someone had asked her to be the thief. Skye had a working relationship with the company—or one of her aliases did, anyway. Despite the fact that HMX had government contracts, she'd worked there undercover in order to gauge if one of their scientists was trying to sell secrets to China. Luckily that scientist hadn't been.

"It took a month of prep work, but I got the right security codes, security passes, and I figured out how to circumvent their actual security. It was tough since I was working alone—sort of, because I did use some assets. They just didn't know they were being used. HMX had holes in their security and I exploited every one of them. I couldn't give him what he wanted—and I never intended to. But telling him no wasn't an option. So I stole the bioweapon, then agreed to meet him at a neutral location. Or so he thought."

Bastard thought he was so smart. And he was, but Skye had been one step ahead of him. *For once.* The man had assumed he'd had her cowed, but he hadn't been able to predict her ultimate plan. Because it was something he never would have done himself.

Taking a deep breath, she continued. "I rigged the place to blow less than thirty seconds after I entered it—which gave me a small but doable escape window. I knew he'd be watching, waiting for me to show up early. He'd want to see if I had backup. So I did what he expected, minus the backup. I'd also laid the groundwork for my 'murder' to trace back to an arms dealer who wanted one of my aliases dead. So it looked real. I used a Jane Doe body I'd stolen from a morgue and I switched out my dental records. He lost the bioweapon and access to me. I've been hunting him ever since my 'death,' but I've had to be careful not to trigger any of his alarms. If he discovered I was still alive..." She shook her head. "So there you have it. I broke a lot of laws, and now you're a party to my crimes." Something she absolutely hated.

Colt was silent for a long moment, watching her. "Who forced you to do this?"

The one thing she didn't want to tell him, but knew she'd have to. It was why she'd left the guy's name out. Because if she'd said it, Colt wouldn't have listened to the details of her story. He'd have simply lost his mind. Because Colt and the man who'd blackmailed her had a history. "Mark Gianni."

Colt's green eyes went mercurial, his jaw clenching tight. "That motherfu—"

"I know. But it's done. And now you know why I have to disappear again." Mark Gianni was one of *them.* Or he had been. He'd retired from the Agency since her "death," then basically fallen off the face of the earth. She had no idea where he was living, not even what country. Because he'd been trained just as well as she had, and he had a hell of a lot more years of experience under his belt. She'd even tried to find out where his pension deposits were going but had run into a dead end. He covered his tracks well.

Colt's jaw flexed. "Why didn't you come to me? Or the director? We would have believed you."

Oh, she knew they'd have believed her. But that wouldn't have mattered. Because Gianni would have gone after Colt, just as he'd promised. He'd found her only weakness and exploited it. She could have gone up against him if it was just her, but if she'd lost Colt it wouldn't have mattered if she'd brought Gianni down. It would have killed her the same as any bullet to the heart.

Skye pulled her hands from his and rubbed the back of her neck. "It's complicated," she muttered.

"What the hell could be so—" He straightened in his chair. "Gianni threatened me, didn't he." Not a question.

She could deny it, but there was no point. Colt had already ripped her open so that she was vulnerable and feeling more raw than she ever had. "Not just you. He knew you better than anyone—he was your recruiter, after all. He sent me pictures of some of your friends. Mary Grace at a clinic she volunteered at, Mercer at one of his pizza joints, Gage Yates at a business meeting. In some high-rise office. In Seattle, I think." The photo had clearly been taken through a long-rage camera. "He wanted to make sure I knew exactly how to hurt you."

"Any other pictures?"

She really didn't want to tell him any more, but knew she had to. "One of you and me—at dinner in Virginia. And one of your dad. He went to a lot of trouble to locate everyone in your life. Or most everyone. The people he could find easily, I suppose." Because there hadn't been pictures of Colt's other three friends, the ones he considered family too. Probably because Gianni hadn't been able to get photos of them. Not with their jobs. Brooks he probably could have gotten if he'd tried, but in the end it hadn't mattered to her, because the threat had been crystal clear and killing four people in Colt's life would have destroyed him.

"What the hell, Skye? You should have told me."

"I *couldn't*. He made it clear he had people in place to kill Mary Grace, Mercer, your dad and Gage if I didn't do as he said. And I *believed* him. He'd have gone after you and me eventually, but he'd have taken the four of them out quickly and viciously. And I didn't know who I could trust at the Agency. I assume he was working alone, but what if he wasn't? What if he had eyes on you? Our boss? And say I did go to you, do you really think we could have gotten people in place to pull Mary Grace, Mercer, Gage, and your dad in time? At the *same* time? If Gianni got wind of it, someone would have died. What if we trusted the wrong person at the Agency and they died because of it?"

"Skye—"

"No! It was the best tactical decision. He never would have expected me to give up my career, my life for you. Because he wouldn't have done it for anyone. And it had to look real." Which meant Colt had to believe she was dead. Him above all else. His reaction had been the one that mattered. "Because if he suspected I faked my death, he'd have followed through on his threats. If he thought I took from him, he'd have made a spectacle of killing your family, then you as payback."

Colt shoved to his feet and started pacing.

Skye braced for his recrimination, for him to tell her how wrong she'd been. And deep down, in a place she didn't want to admit existed, she was terrified that this was when he would leave, tell her *adios*. Way too many people in his life were targets. She wouldn't blame him either.

"You made the right choice," he said, finally stopping and turning back to her. "I wasn't in your shoes and I hate what you did, but…you made the right choice. I won't be a Monday morning quarterback. Not for this."

She stood then, her heart aching even though she'd dreaded this moment was coming. That she'd eventually have to leave him. She should have just left after Saltillo, but she'd selfishly wanted a little longer with him. Because she only had so much strength when it came to him. "I'm glad you understand. I'll leave—"

"You're not going anywhere."

She stopped, blinked at him. "What? You just said I made the right choice."

"You did. Then. But the situation has changed. Gianni thinks you're dead and he doesn't have people in place to hurt my family anymore. And you have people to support you now. We're in front of this—and we're going to hunt that bastard down."

Relief flooded her system that he wasn't leaving. Skye wanted to tell him no. That she could just disappear again. But she was exhausted with hiding out and she knew she couldn't live the rest of her life that way. Eventually, she would be found out. And so far, she wasn't making much progress finding Gianni on her own. Maybe she never would—or maybe he'd find her first. "I should tell you no."

"But you won't." Colt sounded so damn sure of himself.

As he should. Because she couldn't walk away from him.

She launched herself at him, wrapping her arms around his neck as he pulled her in for a tight embrace. The sense of relief was so overpowering it made her dizzy. For the first time in ages, the constant weight pressing her into the ground eased off and she could breathe.

All because of Colt. A man she was pretty sure she didn't deserve. But she wanted to keep him all the same.

CHAPTER TWELVE

—When you show up with a dead body, a real friend
grabs a shovel and doesn't ask questions.—

David had always known his brother, Rafael, was unbal-
anced, but he'd always felt loyalty to him because of their
blood relation. That had been ingrained in him by his father.
Blood matters. Family matters. It's all you have in this world.

His father was dead, and now his brother was close to it.
And David cared nothing about the man in front of him drip-
ping blood onto the dirt and grass on the field where he would
take his last breath.

White clouds streaked across the bright blue sky, the
peaceful day incongruous with the rage burning inside him.

On his knees, his hands bound behind his back, Rafael
stared out sightlessly into the distance and David wondered if
his brother was too far gone from the pain of the torture he'd
inflicted. David hadn't planned to torture him originally. No,
he'd planned to have his brother assassinated and pin it on
someone else. It would have been an easy way to eliminate
what he knew was a threat to his power. But after hearing
those tapes the CIA agent had given him, David had decided
he would make an example of Rafael.

It was one thing to plan a coup, to take over. David still
would have killed him for that—and because he knew his
brother had killed their father—but Rafael had planned to
rape his wife and kill his children. He'd been descriptive in his

intentions, especially toward David's beautiful Maja. For that, Rafael needed to suffer.

"This is what happens when you betray me." He didn't raise his voice, just scanned the dozen men standing in front of them. These were his closest allies, and while he didn't doubt their loyalty, this would be a reminder to all of them and they would tell others.

Soon news would trickle down into the organization that David Ramirez had tortured and killed his own brother. If he could kill his own brother in such a way, then he could kill anyone. One day, far in the future, he wanted to be legitimate, to leave this ugly world behind. His wife and children deserved that legitimacy. Until then, he had to be ruthless, brutal.

He moved a few steps until he was standing behind his brother. He grabbed Rafael by the hair and wrenched his head back. He'd killed with his own hands before. Not as many as Rafael and only when necessary. Though he hated that it had come to this, he struck hard and slit Rafael's throat in one clean slice. Disgust spread through him that his brother had made him do this, that things had ever come this far. If he hadn't been such an absolute psychopath, they could have ruled together. And made a lot of money.

David kicked his brother in the back. Dust whooshed out under the impact of Rafael's body hitting the ground. Blood pooled into the dirt, spreading even as it soaked into the ground.

"I believe all of you here to be loyal, but there is no room for error now. With my father gone we have to put on a strong front. We have to be united if we want to keep our territory. Our enemies are looking for any way to bring us down, to take what's ours, to creep into our territory. Is that what you want?"

Some shook their heads, others just watched him with neutral expressions. "Is there anything anyone needs to tell me? Speak now." He wanted to put this behind him. Especially since he had multiple meetings with his distributors soon. There hadn't been any issues since his father's death, but his brother had started whispering to some of his distributors, questioning David's ability to lead. He would squash those fears, if they existed, today. Then it would be business as usual.

One of his men, Alonso, took a step forward, separating himself from the others. "Two of Rafael's closest guys—Jorge and Enzo—have disappeared. I sent someone to pick them up when you called this meeting. They haven't been located, and..." He cleared his throat. "According to the text I just received, there was info about the female doctor's home residence at Enzo's house. Her address was scrawled on a sticky note. No other details, just the address and her name."

Damn it. Rafael had gone behind his back and likely sent someone after the doctor. Of course he had. Why should David be surprised? Even in death, his brother was trying to screw him over. It had always been the same thing with them since they were kids. David didn't understand it either. They'd had the same opportunities, the same chance at good schools, but it was never enough for Rafael. He'd always wanted to one-up David. Always. And now this.

David nodded once, burying the rage he felt. "Come with me. Everyone else, back to work. And someone dispose of the body. Burn it, bury it, I don't care. Just make sure it disappears." He never wanted to see or think about his brother again. From this day forward, Rafael would not exist in his memory. He had to shove back the words he'd heard his brother saying about what he wanted to do to his wife. It was likely paranoid but he'd added more guards to her after hearing those recordings. Maja and their children were everything to him.

The others nodded and two immediately went to retrieve the corpse while Alonso hurried over to David. "Should I call one of our guys in Texas, have them send someone to the address and cut off Rafael's guys?"

"I'll make the call myself." And he also planned to call one of his government contacts and see if he could get in touch with the CIA. When his father had been alive, he'd had contacts in the US, but David didn't share those same ones. At least not within the CIA. David's were in the DEA, and he didn't want to involve them in this. They might be dirty agents, but he only used them when required and he didn't like them knowing his business any more than necessary.

He'd learned from his father that the CIA worked in shades of gray. He needed to get ahold of that agent he'd talked to, and make it clear he hadn't sent the two men after the doctor. If he could kill Rafael's guys first, it would go a long way toward proving his innocence.

He said a silent prayer to a God he doubted was listening, that he was able to stop those men before they shed innocent blood. Because if they did, he had no doubt the man with the icy green eyes would make sure that David's entire family was killed.

* * *

Zac Savage scanned the neighborhood as he pulled his rental up to Mercer and Mary Grace's house. The house they'd bought was a big Victorian—because they'd both wanted to fill it up with kids. Looked as if they'd get that chance after all. Something Zac was eternally grateful for. He might not have had the best example of what a good mother was, not from his real mom anyway, but he knew Mary Grace and Mercer were going to be incredible parents.

Sliding his earpiece in, he answered his phone when it buzzed in his pocket.

"Hey, what the hell is going on?" Leighton Cannon, one of his childhood friends, asked before he could get a word in. "I just got off the phone with Brooks. Mary Grace is alive! Colt is in Mexico with no backup! Oh and MG's pregnant! What. The. Hell. I go dark for a week and—"

"You've got to slow down, Cannon."

Cannon was in a similar line of work as Zac, and went dark for weeks at a time. "Yeah, sorry. I haven't slept in...three days, maybe. I don't even know what day of the week it is."

"Thursday." Zac stepped from the vehicle and quickly scanned the quiet neighborhood where everyone had large yards and lots of space between the houses. Nothing seemed out of the ordinary but that didn't mean shit. It was after dark and about an hour after most people with office jobs would have gotten home so it was quiet. He opened the garage door using the remote Mercer had given him.

"Where are you? Brooks said you'd headed out for something." The sound of a female voice over a loudspeaker announcing a change in a flight gate came over the phone—in various languages, though the first was German.

"I'm at Mary Grace and Mercer's place, grabbing clothes and other things for Mary Grace." He shut the garage door behind him, stepped inside and disarmed the security system. "Just in case it's not safe we didn't want either of them coming back here."

"Bet Mercer was annoyed."

"Nah. As long as no one tries to separate him from MG, he's letting everything else go. He's like a new man. Even shaved that hideous beard off so he looks like his old self."

"God, I still can't believe she's... I'm so glad." A touch of raw emotion bled through Cannon's words.

No surprise either. All of them had mourned deeply when they thought they'd lost her. It had been like losing a sister.

"So when are you getting in town?" he asked, heading up the stairs. Pictures lined the wall: of Mercer playing ball; of his and Mary Grace's wedding; and more than a handful of the seven of them in various stages throughout the years. The sight made him smile. Other than his grandmother, these people were the only true family he had.

The house was quiet in the way that told him it was truly empty. And he'd entered enough homes and other buildings he wasn't supposed to be in to know. Empty places had a distinctive feel to them.

"By tomorrow morning, I hope. The afternoon at the latest. I'm flying out of— I'll be there as soon as I can. I'm trying to get an earlier flight but it's not looking great."

"You'll get here when you get here." Zac stepped into their bedroom and pulled out a duffel bag from where Mercer said it would be. Since he hadn't changed a damn thing when MG "died," all her stuff was luckily still here.

"So what's going on with Colt?"

"He was supposed to fly back with us this morning, but he and the woman he's with had to stop and get something. Something important, apparently. They said they'd be here later tonight." Which would be in a couple hours. Zac started grabbing things from MG's list, but froze when he realized he needed to get all her...undergarments too. "Shit."

"What?"

"Nothing." He just felt weird pulling her bras and other stuff out of her drawers. So he just reached into the top drawer and grabbed everything. "All right. I've got my phone turned on for at least the next hour. But I'll have internet access on the plane, so if anything changes, email me. Vague is fine. I'll meet you guys at Brooks's."

"You want me to pick you up from the airport?"

"No. Stay close to MG. I'll grab a rental or a cab."

"Good. See you then. I've missed you." Not something he said to many people, but Cannon was definitely one of them.

"Missed you too, brother. I uh, I'll be taking some down time for a while, so if you're not headed out for a job soon after this, let's set up a fishing trip."

Cannon loved fishing. Zac tolerated it, but he liked beer and hanging out with his friend. And downtime sounded a lot like "quitting" Cannon's current profession. Something they'd talk about later. In person. "Sounds good."

Once they disconnected, Zac finished packing and hefted the duffel off the bed. And then he heard the faint splintering of breaking glass. From downstairs.

Easing the bag back down, he withdrew his pistol from his side holster and stepped quietly toward the half-open door. A grunt followed, then a sound of footsteps. If he had to guess the exact location, Zac was betting on the kitchen, since it would be the best place to enter undetected by neighbors' prying eyes. He silently moved the duffel bag under the bed and made sure it was out of sight. He didn't want to leave any trace that someone was here.

He could call the cops. But he wasn't a regular civilian and that wasn't happening. He was going to eliminate whatever this threat was to Mary Grace and Mercer. Unless it was some teenage assholes breaking in—then yeah, he'd call the cops—but the timing of this was way too coincidental.

He silently stepped to the doorway and peered out into the hall. Footsteps carried up the steps, clunking on the wooden stairs. Definitely not a pro—no, it was two people at least. The sets of footsteps were distinctive, one heavier than the other. Maybe they were trying to be quiet but if so, they were doing a terrible job.

From his position, he could see the top of a dark head rising from the staircase into his line of sight. Hispanic man wearing jeans and a long-sleeved T-shirt. Armed. One weapon tucked into the back of his pants, another held loosely at his side.

Zac moved back as another head came into view and the first man started turning in Zac's direction. He took another step back, then another before ducking into the walk-in closet. He left the light off and the door ajar enough to see out. There were a lot of windows in this room, letting in enough moonlight that he could see fine.

The closet would have to do as his hiding spot. He'd disarm and neutralize.

"*Hay un carro afuera,*" someone whispered.

"*¿Ves u oyes a alguien? No. Esperamos que regresen. Mátalos limpio y rápido. Revisa ese cuarto. Yo reviso este.*"

These assholes thought they could kill Zac's friends? Oh, these morons were about to die. He didn't relish killing people, despite his "Savage" moniker. But he wouldn't let these guys anywhere near his friends. A moment later the first man he'd seen on the stairs entered the bedroom, his gaze sweeping over the bed, dresser, and the little nook with all the windows and sheer curtains.

When he stepped into the bathroom, Zac tucked his pistol away and stepped out of the closet. Though his heart rate had increased slightly, he kept calm. This was something he'd done before and would likely do again.

In his peripheral vision, Zac watched the halfway open door and moved quickly to the wall next to the bathroom. The position blocked him from view of anyone moving down the hallway, and it would let him attack this intruder with an element of surprise. He didn't want to use his weapon because he wanted as much silence as possible.

Moments later, the man stepped out, his weapon *still* held down at his side. Unprofessional was what it was. He wasn't even properly clearing a room.

Zac moved with trained precision, his body drawing on muscle memory as he grabbed the wrist of the weapon hand, yanked hard, snapped it even as he looped his other arm around the guy's neck. The man sucked in air, making a gasping sound as the weapon fell to the floor with an unavoidable thud. Zac pulled him back tight against his chest, increasing pressure around his neck, using all the strength in his body to immobilize him.

The man struggled, flailed, grasping desperately with his one good hand, digging into Zac's forearm. Adrenaline pumping, Zac repositioned his other hand, and quickly snapped the guy's neck. It took force, but not as much as most people assumed. Of course most victims didn't just lie there and let you break their neck so it did take strength to initially subdue someone.

"Enzo?" a male voice faintly called out as Zac dragged the body back into the bathroom.

As he did, Zac saw a familiar tattoo on the man's neck, showing off his violent history through symbols of the gang he belonged to—one widely known to work with the Ramirez cartel. Two of the symbols Zac recognized, and they stood for murder and rape.

One down. One to go.

CHAPTER THIRTEEN

—Social awkwardness is my superpower.—

Colt glanced over at Skye, squeezed her hand as the civilian cargo plane they were sitting in started its final descent. They both had on ear protection because of the lack of insulation, unlike the private plane his friends had flown home in. He and Skye had decided to come later.

She'd needed to pick up the flash drive she had with all her files on Gianni, which had added a couple extra hours to their trip. She hadn't wanted to fly in with everyone anyway. She was worried Gianni might have someone watching Mercer and Mary Grace, and Colt hadn't balked at keeping distance from them for the flight home. Just in case, he wanted to take all precautions. Which meant he'd have to go see his dad when he got home, but he'd think about that later.

Now he just needed to find where the hell Gianni was. Once Colt had him in his sights, the man was dead. Their past, all their history—it made this betrayal brutal. And Colt was going to make him pay. There would be no arrest, no jail time. He would kill the bastard. He didn't plan to get caught, but if he did, going to jail would be worth it.

Skye gave him a wary smile as they touched down in Redemption Harbor. He knew she was nervous about bringing other people into this, but hell, Mercer had been right when he'd told Colt no more lone ranger shit. Both he and Skye could stand to depend on people more often. Right now was definitely one of those times.

Especially against someone like Mark Gianni. About two decades older than Colt, the man had been very, very good at his job. Colt had never truly trusted him—that had been something Gianni grilled into him when he'd recruited Colt. Don't trust anyone, not even him. But Colt had never thought Gianni could be capable of this. Of going after Colt's friends, his family—of targeting the woman he loved, forcing her to steal a bioweapon for him.

He pulled his cell phone from his pocket and turned it on. Immediately he got pings, indicating multiple texts and voicemails. Most were from Mercer and Savage, but one was from Agent Lewis. The message was simple: *Call me.*

Lewis had done him a huge favor by giving him David Ramirez's location, so he'd have to call him back immediately.

Everything okay? Skye mouthed as the plane slowed, then stopped.

He nodded as the engines cut off. They both took off their ear coverings and unstrapped from the only two jump seats at the front of the plane. "I've got to call Lewis back," he said. "Not sure what it's about."

Skye nodded as Vienna, their pilot—also an occasional smuggler of fine art—ducked into the back. Her midnight black hair was pulled back from her face, her headset loose around her neck. "The flight okay?"

"We're good. Thank you for bringing us here," Skye said. Before leaving Corpus Christi, she'd donned the disguise she'd had on in Saltillo so her appearance was slightly altered. And thanks to Vienna, they'd be bypassing security.

"Thank you for those sweet weapons." Vienna's grin was wide and infectious. "My brother's going to be jealous."

Skye had given her a couple custom-made pistols, even though Colt had told her that he would simply pay Vienna, a woman he'd worked with before. But Skye had been typically stubborn and insisted on "paying for this" since he was helping her out. As if he needed anything from her as payment. But he'd let her have her way.

"Call me if you ever need a pilot," Vienna said. "You guys should be good to go. You need a ride anywhere from the airport? I'm staying in Redemption Harbor for a few days."

"No," he said, not wanting to pull his contact into anything with them. She didn't even know he was CIA, just thought he was an art thief. "But thanks. I've got someone picking us up." He was glad to be home, even if the circumstances were less than ideal.

She nodded once. "Good stuff. If you're hungry stop by Dancing Dragon and tell Hwan I sent you. You'll eat for free."

Skye gave her a real smile. "Thanks. Maybe we will."

It was doubtful they would, but Colt could tell Skye genuinely liked Vienna. After exiting the plane, they left the private airport on foot, not stopping until they reached a hotel a mile away. They didn't go inside, however, just sat on one of the benches under the parking overhang.

"I'll order a taxi while you call that agent back," Skye murmured, glancing up as a couple holding hands strode past them without a sideways glance. Even though she'd changed her appearance she'd added sunglasses and a ball cap.

He'd done the same. Nodding, he pulled out the burner Agent Arthur Lewis had been using to contact him.

"Hey, about time," Lewis said. "I just had a very interesting conversation with our boss."

Oh, hell.

Before Colt could think about responding, Lewis continued. "Turns out David Ramirez just got in contact with Director Hernandez—he wanted to make it clear that he had nothing to do with the men sent after Mary Grace Jackson and family. And the director had no idea what he was talking about, much less why the new leader of the Ramirez cartel was calling him. But he played along."

Colt's blood iced over. "Someone went after Mary Grace again?"

"Are you hearing me? The director knows you're not on vacation now, and—"

Yeah, because he cared about that. "Have you tried contacting either of the Jacksons?"

A pause. "Tried the husband. Couldn't get an answer, though I did get a location of his phone. It's not at the house they own. You need to talk to Hernandez now."

Next to Colt, he was aware of Skye making a call, most definitely to Mercer since she had his number now. "Fine, I'll call him."

"No. I'm connecting you. I have strict orders..." Colt tuned Lewis out as Skye shook her head and set her phone down.

A few seconds later, Hernandez's quiet, deep voice came over the line. "So, you're not on vacation?"

"I got pulled into something," he said, standing because he couldn't sit still any longer. The cab should be there soon anyway.

"Your line secure?"

"Yeah," Colt said, feeling helpless as he waited. He needed to talk to Mary Grace and Mercer, to know they were all right.

"So what did you get pulled into?"

"I can't talk about it right now. What happened with Ramirez?"

"I still don't know. But whatever it was you said to him, you scared the shit out of the man. We'll be able to work with him in the future—and he killed his brother."

Colt blinked at that, surprised it had happened so quickly. "Yeah?"

"He didn't tell me, but word has spread through his organization. He made an example out of Rafael. From what I understand, David Ramirez then learned that his brother had already sent people after the Jackson family. What the hell is going on? That woman was supposed to be dead. Now she's not. She was rescued by an unknown individual and now *David Ramirez* is reaching out to *me?* I want answers and I want you back in DC ASAP."

"I can't, sir. Give me two hours and I'll contact you with more information. I'm on to something big...can you trust me? I've never let you down before."

Hernandez was silent for a long moment. Then, "You've got two hours." He disconnected without saying anything else, which wasn't a surprise.

Colt dialed Mercer as the cab pulled up. Skye, her backpack still on, raced to the door and held it open for him. No one answered. Next he tried Savage. No answer either.

"I couldn't get through either," Skye said after she gave the driver the address.

Colt simply nodded and took her hand in his. They couldn't talk any more details in front of a stranger anyway. Now all he could do was hope he got hold of his friends before they reached Brooks's house—and pray that the worst hadn't happened.

Halfway to Brooks's estate, Colt received a text from Mercer. *Got a problem. We'll deal with it when you get here.*

Colt showed the phone to Skye, who simply frowned, the worry in her eyes clear.

He texted back. *Everyone okay?* Meaning, was everyone alive.

Yes. We're all good.

Relief punched through him. Okay, he could wait a little bit longer. Not that he had a choice.

* * *

"Are you ready?" Colt looked at Skye as they stepped up onto the front porch of Brooks's home. She held on to the straps of her backpack as if she was using them as a lifeline. The action was so out of character for the strong woman he knew. Nothing ever fazed her. But after what she'd told him about that bastard Gianni, he was surprised how well she'd been holding up with no backup until now.

"No."

Before she had a chance to say anything else, the door flew open.

Mercer rushed out and pulled Skye into a bear hug, lifting her off the ground a couple inches. Her entire body jolted, and for a moment, Colt thought she was going to push him off, but instead she shot Colt a confused look before awkwardly patting Mercer on the back. "Nice to meet you, dude."

When Mercer pulled back, he gave her the biggest smile. "I'm happy to meet the woman who gave me back my wife."

Mercer turned to him before Skye could respond and pulled him into a rib-crushing hug as well. Then Mercer slapped him on the back hard enough to make him take a step forward. "I'm still pissed at you for leaving me behind but..I love you, man. There are no words for how grateful I'll always be."

Colt just nodded and wrapped an arm around Skye's shoulders. "You'd have done the same thing. Even though you've already tackle-hugged her, this is officially Skye. She's my girl. And we're going to assist her with a problem."

"Or, I could just disappear and handle this on my own," she muttered.

Colt squeezed her shoulders once. They'd gone back and forth on this before the plane ride even though she'd originally agreed to his help in the Corpus Christi motel. But in the end he knew she would accept what they were offering. She'd come this far. "What's going on?" he asked Mercer. "Your text was vague and you didn't answer your phone."

"Yeah. Sorry about that. Didn't have it on me because we were trying to figure out what to do. Everyone's at the back of the house. There's an issue." Mercer's expression darkened.

"SITREP?" he asked out of habit. Mercer might not have been former military, but he understood Colt's language.

"Two dead bodies."

"Who?" he asked as they followed Mercer into the huge ranch house. It was all wood, stone and a lot of natural light during the daytime.

"Don't know. Savage went to our house to pick up some clothes for Mary Grace and two guys showed up. Both speaking Spanish—planning to kill us—both with gang tattoos he says link them to the Ramirez cartel."

Well that made sense, considering what Lewis had told him. He figured he knew the answer, but... "Anyone call the cops?"

Mercer snorted as they stepped out onto the back lanai overlooking the Olympic-sized pool—which was lit up with multi-color lights. Strategically placed solar lights were situated all around the pool, built-in hot tub and the five-foot wrought iron and red brick fencing. Everyone was there except Leighton. "No. You told us to lie low, so we're lying low.

MG's not too happy about not calling them, but..." He lifted a shoulder as everyone grew silent and turned to look at them.

"Why's she standing?" Skye asked, giving Mercer an admonishing look. "She shouldn't be on her feet."

"Oh my God, you're more ridiculous than my husband," Mary Grace said, crossing the short distance and pulling Skye into another awkward hug. "I'm pregnant, not broken."

"I think she's right." Mercer wrapped his arms around Mary Grace as if she were made of glass and led her to the oversized rectangle table the others had been standing by, likely discussing the apparent corpses that had to be somewhere nearby.

Mary Grace sat down, looking beyond exasperated even as she patted her husband's hand.

"Everyone, this is Skye," Colt said, wanting to get the introductions out of the way. Then they had stuff to discuss.

She nodded as everyone introduced themselves, then half-smiled at Savage. "Nice to see you again."

Colt frowned, looking between the two of them. He knew they'd worked a job together, sort of, years before he'd met Skye. For reasons he understood completely, he was feeling raw and territorial about her. He shifted a step closer to Skye, not liking the little smirk that played across Savage's face as he tracked Colt's movements.

"You want to pee a circle around me?" she murmured low enough for only him to hear, clearly catching on to his mood.

Her words eased something inside him and he didn't bother to fight his grin. "Maybe I will." He cleared his throat. "So, the bodies—"

"Do you have pigs on this farm?" Skye asked.

Brooks nodded. "Yeah, why?"

Savage just snorted as Gage's eyes widened, both of them clearly catching on to her meaning. Colt was surprised Brooks didn't get her meaning.

She lifted a shoulder, looking uncomfortable. "What? Pigs will eat anything. If we want to dispose of the bodies, it's the best way given our current situation."

Colt cleared his throat as everyone stared at her for a moment.

"I like that idea," Savage said as Mary Grace gasped.

Mary Grace shook her head. "We should call the police."

"No, we shouldn't." Colt shook his head. "According to my contact, only two men were sent after you. We'll just make them disappear. No paperwork for the locals, none for my guys, and no media shitstorm for you. For now we're going to keep your reappearance quiet, but eventually it will come out. We'll all shield you as much as possible, but adding two dead gang members found in your house? We can't afford any extra spotlight right now. Not to mention Ramirez might change his mind if it hits the media that you took out his brother's men." David might not have sent them, but if the guy decided he needed to save face, who knew what he might do. No, it was better if these two thugs disappeared.

"It just feels wrong," she said, a frown pulling at her lips.

"Well they would have killed you and Mercer with no compunction. I'll make them disappear. No one else needs to be involved." He loved his friends, but right now this wasn't a democracy. He needed to deal with the threat after Skye, and two dead bodies would slow things down once local law enforcement got involved. And forget about the media. That type of unwanted attention was the last thing they needed. "We've got other stuff to deal with. First, I think these were the only two guys sent after you. Rafael Ramirez sent them before his brother killed him."

Mary Grace's eyes widened. "He's dead?"

"Yep. Now on to Skye's problem." He pulled her close to him, thankful when she sank against him as if she belonged there. "I think we should all take a seat."

It took twenty minutes for him to outline the problem of Mark Gianni.

"So how well do you know this Gianni guy?" Gage asked, the first to speak when Colt finished.

"He was my recruiter." And now all his friends knew who he worked for. He was breaking a whole lot of rules by telling them, but he didn't care. Skye's well-being was the only thing that mattered. "My friend at one point. Or I thought he was."

"Damn," Savage muttered.

"And this bastard had pictures of all of us?" Gage asked, a calculating gleam in his bluish-gray eyes.

"Except for Savage and Leighton," Colt confirmed. Because of the nature of their covert work, it had probably been impossible for him to get pictures of them. "Oh, and Brooks." Which could be for a number of reasons. Maybe because Brooks would have been more likely to notice someone tailing him. Or maybe Gianni had thought that threatening four people was enough to scare Skye into doing what he wanted.

"You need to talk to your dad too," Mercer added.

"I know." Colt just wasn't looking forward to seeing his father. They had...a complicated relationship. "I'll go over in a bit. Skye will stay with you."

"Um, Skye is right here and she's going with you." She looked at him as if he'd lost his mind. Then she slid her flash drive over to Gage. "Colt says you're a genius with computers. I've got skills, but Gianni is careful. I covertly searched for him, but with him thinking I was dead, I couldn't afford to trigger any online traps he might have set up. So I don't have much on him. His basics are here though. Should give you somewhere to start."

Gage palmed the drive and gave that same sly grin as before. "I'm definitely going to find this guy."

"Then what do we do?" Mary Grace asked.

Colt shot Skye a glance. She gave him a hard look in return. They'd talked about this before coming here. He wanted to go after Gianni, take him out. But she wanted to let the Agency take over now that she knew all of Colt's friends and family were safe. He knew why too. She didn't want him to get hurt, but Colt wasn't concerned for himself. No, he knew how the Agency worked. If Gianni promised them something good enough, they could let him walk. Or give him a reduced sentence. Either way, the guy wouldn't be dead. Which would put Skye in danger all over again.

No, Colt knew *exactly* how the Agency worked. In shades of gray. Which was normally fine with him. Sometimes the greater good truly did matter. But sometimes...letting a monster go free because he offered information on another monster didn't balance out.

And even if it did, Colt wouldn't risk the Agency screwing things up and Skye getting hurt. Nope. Not happening. There was pretty much no rule he wouldn't break to keep her alive and safe.

"I just want to find him," Colt finally said, turning back to his friends. "We'll figure it out from there."

Skye crossed her arms over her chest and leaned back in her seat. "No, you want to bait him." He should have known she wouldn't let this go.

He sighed. "It's the best plan. He doesn't know you're alive, and if I reach out to him with news that you might be, I can lead him in the direction we want him to go. We just need

Gage to figure out where he is first so we can get eyes on him, start watching him."

"If he was your recruiter and you parted on good terms...it would make sense for you to reach out to him about something like this," Savage said.

Skye's expression darkened. "I don't like it."

"Yeah, well I didn't like you faking your own death. So we'll just agree to disagree."

"Jackass," she muttered.

Gage laughed lightly and stood. "I like her, Colt. And I'm going to start working my magic. I'm staying here for the time being too. We all are."

"The blue bedroom upstairs is free if you guys want it. You'll have your own bathroom too," Brooks added.

Colt was glad everyone was staying here. The ranch was on almost a thousand acres and Brooks had top-of-the-line security so if anyone tried to infiltrate the land, they'd know about it—and could take the right measures to end any threat. "Thanks, brother." He stood and pulled Gage into a hug, grateful for his friends and that he could call on them like this. Though Gage hadn't said it, it was clear he'd taken off work for this.

"You know it. We're going to get this guy, Skye." Gage squeezed her shoulder in a friendly manner before heading inside the house.

Something in Colt's chest tightened at the way his friends—his family—had accepted her and this situation so easily. Not that he was surprised. She'd literally faked her death because she hadn't wanted them to get killed. Yeah, it had been for him, but she'd made a sacrifice for virtual strangers. Hard not to want to help someone like that.

"Why don't you guys head inside, take a shower? I know you've been traveling all day," Brooks said as he stood. "We've got all the details now, and with Gage working on finding Gianni there's not a lot we can do. And if we are going to go after him, we're going to need to be sharp."

"What about the bodies?" Colt wanted to take care of that before anything else. Those guys needed to get disappeared fast.

"I can take care of it." Savage stood, rolling his shoulders once.

Colt wanted to insist on helping, but when he looked at Skye and saw the fatigue playing across her features, he simply nodded. Brooks was right. They needed rest, then they could regroup. And he needed to call his boss back before the two-hour mark was up.

Then he needed to head out and visit his dad. Something he wasn't looking forward to. "All right. Think you could whip us up some pizzas?" he asked Mercer.

His friend grinned. "Hell, yeah. Be back in the kitchen in an hour. I'll feed everyone."

"I'll be gone a little longer," Savage said. "You better save me some food."

"I'll make sure there's food for you." Taking Skye's hand, Colt stood and pulled her close to him.

She didn't resist, just leaned against him in a way that told him she trusted him. That knowledge eased most of the tension in his shoulders. They might be going up against a ruthless bastard, but if they worked as a team, he knew they'd win. They just had to.

CHAPTER FOURTEEN

—You are my North Star.—

Even though Colt wanted to be in the shower with Skye, he waited until he heard the water running before calling his boss. Hernandez wasn't going to like what he had to say, but he'd just have to deal with it.

"You on your way to DC?" the man asked, his way of answering.

"No, and I'm not coming back yet."

"Colt—"

"I get that you're pissed, but I brought you David Ramirez on a platter. His brother is dead, which is what everyone wanted. Now he's got a healthy dose of fear for us. Which means he'll potentially work with Lewis's division. Also what everyone wanted. I did all that during my vacation. I heard a rumor about my friend being held captive by the cartel—which she was. I went to Mexico on my own dime without using company resources." Yeah, technically there was a ban on US personnel traveling in certain regions, but that didn't exactly apply to him. "Now I'm dealing with something that doesn't require any backup. Yet. If and when it does, I'll contact you. Until then, I'm taking the rest of my vacation or you can fire me."

His boss was silent for so long that Colt checked the screen to see if they were still connected. It said a lot for how he felt at this point in his life that losing his job wasn't the worst thing in the world. At one time, the thought of losing his status at the Agency, of not being able to do what he did, would have screwed up his entire world. Now, the only thing he was scared of losing was Skye.

"If you fuck up, I'm not coming after you. You'll be on your own. Got it?"

"Yep."

"Good. If I don't hear from you before your vacation is up, be in my office at seven your first day back."

"Will do."

His boss disconnected and Colt set the phone on the nightstand as he collapsed onto the queen-sized guest bed. This place was huge, with more than enough rooms to accommodate everyone. Brooks's father had handed the place over to him a few years ago and spent most of his time in Florida with his new wife—who was younger than Brooks. So no one would bother them at least.

Taking off his shoes and shirt, he fell back against the overstuffed pillows and rubbed a hand over his face. The thought of baiting his recruiter, the man who'd trained him, treated him like family... He knew Skye hadn't lied about Gianni threatening his friends and family. But how had it come to this? How had the man who'd recruited him turned without him noticing? He was trained to look out for shit like this.

Apparently Colt had a blind spot.

At the sound of the bathroom door opening, he automatically swiveled toward it—and his breath caught in his throat.

Skye stood there, completely naked, her damp hair down around her shoulders. She'd washed the temporary color out and the contacts were gone, so this was all her.

The woman he'd fallen in love with faster than he'd ever thought possible. Hell, he'd never even had a chance. Not falling for her was an impossibility.

Hunger surged through him as he drank in the sight of all her bare skin, the sleek, lean lines of her toned body and perfect light brown nipples. Just like that, he was hard, his entire body reacting to her with an unparalleled intensity.

Whatever the future had in store for them, it could wait a little bit longer.

CHAPTER FIFTEEN

—I'm yours. Now and always.—

Skye knew that she and Colt had things to do, and should get rest, but...she also knew they needed this more. Especially him.

The pressure of everything, of basically hunting down his recruiter, a man he'd once respected, was weighing on him. Even if he hadn't said it, she knew him, could see it in his expression even though he tried to hide it.

"Get naked," she murmured, striding toward him where he sat on the bed. This was happening right now because the truth was, she needed him inside her. Needed to feel bonded to him even more, especially after all those months apart. It had been as if she'd lost a part of herself. Before him she'd kept her life compartmentalized, all neat and tidy. Then he'd disrupted it.

His eyes went molten as he drank her in from head to toe. She'd missed that look, that visible hunger from him she felt all the way to her core.

She'd been too afraid to look into him too much while they'd been apart, to check up on him, for multiple reasons. If he'd moved on from her, found someone else in the last six months? It would have destroyed her. Especially since she couldn't fathom moving on from him. No one compared.

He'd fully stripped by the time she reached the bed, every glorious inch of his hard body exposed. The lamp on the nightstand was on, casting a soft glow over his muscles and thick, full erection. *Yes, please.*

He let out a low growling sound as she crawled onto the bed and slid on top of him.

Looking down at him, she spread her hands over his chest, wanting to tell him so much, to express how much he meant to her. He was willing to go to such drastic lengths to help her and that meant everything to her. She couldn't find the words to tell him, however. No, the words stuck in her throat. Because she'd never felt as if she deserved him. She wasn't sweet or compassionate like Mary Grace, and the thought of kids or a family terrified her. Colt deserved something like that. Instead he'd gotten her. A woman who could accurately hit a target the size of a playing card at a thousand yards—consistently.

"What are you thinking right now?" He shifted, sitting up slightly so that his cock lay heavy between them as he cupped her cheek with his callused hand.

Damn it, she couldn't find her voice. After crying in that motel it was as if something had broken free inside her. She didn't like it, and she wanted to shove it right back where it had come from.

Leaning forward, she meant to kiss him softly, gently, but the second their lips touched, a raw hunger consumed her. Something wild sparked between them as she teased her tongue into his mouth. Damn it, she'd meant to be seductive, to take things slow and kiss every inch of his delicious body, working from his cock upward.

That wasn't happening now.

Heat flooded her core as he gripped one of her hips hard and slid his fingers through her damp hair, holding her head tight. She loved the way he held on to her, as if afraid to let go.

She didn't want to let go of him either. Once had been hard enough. Harder than losing her parents. Colt was in her blood, her soul. Even if she couldn't always find the words she needed to express that.

Lifting up slightly, she rubbed her already slick folds along the length of his erection, shuddering as the head of his cock slid over her clit. She wanted him inside her, but she wanted to build anticipation just a little. Because heavy foreplay simply wasn't happening now.

The energy humming through him was a live thing, his body practically vibrating beneath her. She moaned into his mouth as he ate at hers, rolling his hips against hers.

Digging her fingers into his shoulders, she clutched tight as she began moving over his erection, rubbing herself against him up and down, the friction against her clit sending pleasure pulsing through her.

He reached between their bodies and cupped her mound. When he slid two fingers inside her without warning, she arched against him, her breasts rubbing against his chest. It was too much and not enough. She needed all of him.

"Hell, yeah," he murmured against her mouth before pulling back slightly to look at her. Keeping his gaze pinned to hers, he shifted his hips until his thick length was positioned right at her opening.

She tried to slide down on him, but he held her immobile, holding her hips tight.

"Mine." The word was a savage growl.

Yours. Now. Always. He owned her, something he had to know. Otherwise she'd never have sacrificed everything for his safety. Still, she couldn't force the word out.

Releasing her hips, he thrust upward, sinking deep inside her. She sucked in a sharp breath as he filled her completely.

She wanted to ride him, but he moved quickly, flipping them so he was on top.

She shouldn't be surprised. Sometimes he had to be in control. And she was okay relinquishing it. Especially now when all his muscles were pulled taut and there was something wild in his green eyes. She recognized that look and savored it.

With his gaze pinned to hers, caging her against the bed with his big body, he pulled almost all the way out, with just the head of his cock at her entrance.

Her inner walls clenched, wanting to be filled by him. "No teasing," she rasped out.

His dark expression said he wasn't teasing. Far from it. "You're not leaving me again." The words seemed to be torn from his throat.

She wanted to tell him that she wouldn't, that she *couldn't* leave him again, but yeah, the words just weren't coming.

Growling, he crushed his mouth to hers again as he thrust hard inside her. She lost herself with him, in the rhythm of their bodies. With her legs and arms wrapped around him as he filled her, she never wanted to let go.

He'd owned her for far longer than she'd ever admitted to him. To herself. She'd tried to keep her distance in the beginning, to deny what she felt for him, what he *made* her feel, damn him. Because the thought of losing *him*, it sliced her up inside.

When his hand reached between their bodies and teased her clit, she was already so far gone that falling over the edge was inevitable. Her orgasm punched through her like a tsunami, sending spiral after spiral of pleasure through her until it was too much.

His own climax followed immediately, and when he emptied himself inside her, she wrapped even tighter around him, holding him close. She never wanted to let him go.

She rubbed her cheek against his, smiling at the feel of his stubble. "You need to shave," she murmured.

"Maybe I'll grow it out."

"Hmm." That could be sexy. Everything he did was.

Groaning slightly, he rolled off her but didn't go far. He stretched out next to her and she curled up to him, throwing a leg over his hips as she buried her face into his chest.

The scent of him was masculine, earthy, and she'd missed it. "I need to say something," she murmured against his skin.

"Okay." He had an arm around her, was idly stroking a hand down her spine.

"I'm...not going to change who I am." She pulled back so she could look at him as she spoke, but didn't put any real distance between them. She just wanted to make sure she had his full attention right now. "The way I was raised shaped me in ways that make me a little different, and I'm okay with that. But I'll probably always have inappropriate suggestions—like feeding dead bodies to pigs instead of freaking out and wanting to call the cops." Mary Grace had looked at Skye with a tad bit of horror and she hated to admit that it bothered her. Because she liked Mary Grace. And now Skye wondered if her suggestion had bothered Colt. Skye had always embraced who she was, but she knew she could be awkward in certain situations. Especially if she let her guard down and was herself around others. It was why she'd had so few friends over the years.

"I don't want you to change. I love who you are. Weirdness and all."

"You say that now—"

"No, I'll say that always. We fit each other. I love that you automatically know how many exits are in any room, that you can build any number of explosive devices with household items—that you carry around C4 the way most women carry around lipstick. I'll always worry about you, because I love you. But because of who you are, I know you can take care of yourself, and that eases something inside me. I like how capable you are. It's one of the sexiest things about you. And the pig thing was a good suggestion. I should have thought of it."

She blinked. "Oh."

"That's it?"

She hadn't expected that answer, but she loved it, and now felt lighter inside somehow. "I like how capable you are too. It's sexy as anything. Even if I can shoot better than you."

He pinched her butt lightly, the grin on his face making her smile in return. She wanted to stay where they were for the rest of the night, but knew they couldn't. There would be very little rest for them. They had too much to do.

"Want me to join you in the shower before we head down to grab food?" After that, they'd go to his father's house, something she knew he wasn't looking forward to.

"Yes, but no. Because we'll never make it if you do that, and I want to get on the road to my dad's soon."

"You're probably right." Though she didn't want to, she pushed up, ready to clean up and get dressed.

But Colt pulled her back to him for a long, hard kiss that she felt all the way to the tips of her toes. Just like the first kiss they'd shared. Only now she was completely bonded to him. There would be no walking away again.

* * *

Mark Gianni used a backdoor channel to slip into the Agency's system. Even though he'd retired, he'd taken a handful of login codes from various coworkers who were none the wiser. Some had changed in the last couple months so he'd lost access with them, but he still had two codes left. If he was ever caught, he'd be sent to prison for life. But he wasn't using a computer linked to him, and unfortunately he was only able to do surface searches because of the lower security clearance levels.

Scanning files, he narrowed in on one linked to the Ramirez cartel. Everything about that rescue was bothering him. Because he didn't know enough about it, and the woman involved was Mary Grace Jackson. But he still had to cover his bases.

His heart rate accelerated when he saw Colt Stuart's name tagged on a file. He'd never worked the Coahuila region or much of Mexico at all. Colt's focus had been on South America, though he'd done some work in the Middle East as well because of his military background.

He opened the file, scanned what he could—because a good portion of it was redacted. He could read through the lines well enough, however.

Colt shouldn't have been in the region at all, but he'd reached out to David Ramirez. For...some reason. He closed the file down, then scanned for any other mention of Stuart and found one about the rescue. Not done by an Agency asset or the Agency. And it was being kept quiet.

Once he was certain there wasn't anything else he could use, he logged out with his stolen credentials, then turned the computer off.

Mark hadn't talked to Colt in months. After Skye's funeral, he'd called him, but Colt had only gotten back to him months later, claiming he'd been busy. After her death, Colt had changed.

Enough time had passed that he should be over her now. Skye had made him weak. To be truly effective, Colt couldn't afford to have any attachments that might hold him back. He was already a star at the Agency and one day, Mark wanted to recruit him to work *with* him.

He was already raking it in and if he ever managed to steal that bioweapon, he'd have enough money to do whatever he wanted once he sold it to the highest bidder. And he knew exactly who would buy it from him: North Korea. Or the Russians. Either one worked for him.

Mark wasn't under any illusions. He knew that Colt wouldn't go total dark side, so he'd have to lie about some of their dealings, convince him that working together would be better than working for the "greater good." At one time Mark had believed in it, but then one of his partners had been captured and the Agency had hung him out to dry. As if all those years of service had meant nothing.

That could have been Mark. It could have been anyone. After that, Mark had just bided his time, waiting until he could retire, taking as much information with him as possible when he did. Because information was power.

It was how he'd forced Skye Arévalo to steal for him, to break her moral code. Almost everyone could be bought. But not someone like her, so he'd had to use leverage. He wouldn't have killed Colt—but he would have killed Colt's friends to get her to do what he wanted. And he'd planned to kill Skye once he'd gotten what he wanted too.

Stepping out onto the terrace from the master bedroom of the villa belonging to his alias Terrence Pace, he breathed in the crisp, night air and the scent of salt from the ocean. After going back and forth he decided to flat out call Colt. Mark needed to find out more about what he'd been doing in Mexico and who the woman was who'd rescued Mary Grace. It was probably no one he knew, but Mark had been in this business a long damn time. He had to watch his own back. Always.

He contemplated calling contacts at the Agency, but he didn't want anyone to know he was asking questions. Calling Colt directly would be the smart thing to do.

Scrolling through the list of numbers he had for Colt, he dialed his Agency phone number using an encrypted phone. Since Colt wouldn't know the number he might not answer. Mark prepared to leave a message.

"Yeah?" Colt answered on the third ring.

"It's Gianni. How are you?"

There was a moment of silence. "Hey...been a long time."

"Yeah."

"Where're you calling from?"

"Oh, this is a new cell number. I'm in Florida."

"Nice. How's retirement?"

"Eh, I keep busy." Colt had no idea just how busy. No one did.

Colt gave a short, easy laugh. "I was surprised when you retired so early. Everything okay?"

"Yeah. I just got off the phone with a buddy from the Agency. Said there was some kind of issue with you and the Ramirez cartel. Said your friend, the doctor, is alive?" He'd known about Mary Grace Jackson being killed months ago and had reached out then as well. Colt had spoken to him, but had been distant as he grieved.

"Who'd you talk to?" Colt asked.

He snorted. "You know I can't tell you that."

There was another pregnant pause. "All right, look, my friend was rescued by a private company. I might have been involved, and much to my boss's annoyance I reached out to the cartel to smooth things over. I'm taking time off to be with her and her husband before heading back in. So you heard right. There was an issue, but I'm okay. And I should have called you back months ago. I got the card and flowers you sent. I appreciate it. I was still struggling with...Skye's death. Then to lose another friend. I wasn't in the best frame of mind."

"I understood. When your name came up, I just wanted to check in and make sure you were okay. If you want to head down to Miami, take a break before going back to work, I've always got a door open for you." He didn't have a place in Florida but he could make last-minute arrangements if Colt took him up on the offer. His main goal was to feel out Colt right now, to understand his frame of mind—and to find out if he was hiding something.

So far he'd detected nothing that alerted his inner radar.

"Thanks, man. I appreciate it."

"How are you doing with Skye's death?" He should be over the bitch by now, but there was no accounting for taste.

"Dealing with it. Look, I've got to go, but send me your info. I'll let you know if I decide to head to Miami before I go back to work."

Once they disconnected, Mark decided he would do a little research of his own. See if he could find out what company had been behind the rescue. Because he couldn't get the details of the attack on the cartel compound out of his mind. He'd seen that kind of destruction before, seen that layout of explosive devices in a very similar pattern—set up to create maximum damage. It could be nothing.

But his instinct was telling him it wasn't.

CHAPTER SIXTEEN

—I hope you never soften your edges.—

"You sounded believable," Skye said to Colt as they hurried down the stairs. She couldn't believe Mark Gianni had just called him. It made her itchy, ready to run again. She wouldn't, but...the instinct was there. "It took all the training I have." His jaw was clenched tight as they entered the kitchen.

Where everyone was already eating homemade pizza. At the scent of baked bread, tomato sauce and oregano, her stomach rumbled and she realized she couldn't remember the last time she'd eaten.

"Gianni just called me." Colt's words made everyone freeze around the long, rectangular, refurbished table.

Gage jumped up immediately. "You got a number or was it unknown?"

"It showed up. I doubt it'll be trackable." He handed his cell phone over to Gage nonetheless.

"Save me some food," he said, racing from the room.

"I'll get you both plates." Mary Grace stood. "Sit, talk and then you can eat."

Mercer took over, refusing to let his wife do anything, and Skye followed Colt's lead, sitting on the long bench across from Mary Grace, Savage and Brooks.

"He know Skye's alive?" Savage asked.

"I don't know. He said he heard about Mary Grace's rescue. From a contact at the Agency."

Skye didn't like the sound of that at all. "It feels like bullshit to me."

"Yeah, agreed." Colt's expression was grim, but he gave Mercer a grateful smile as he placed plates in front of them. "That's not the kind of thing that gets brought up in conversation. So my guess is he has access to files he shouldn't have. Which could mean someone's feeding him information or he hacked the system."

"What did he want?" Savage asked.

"I think he was fishing for information. But he called to 'check up on me.' After MG's death he sent condolence flowers and a card. He did the same thing for Skye."

Skye placed a calming hand on his flexed forearm, needing to soothe him. She wanted to break Gianni's face in half, but they needed to be calm now. To think rationally and take him down the right way.

He took a calming breath, set his hand over hers and squeezed gently. "I told him a private company was hired to rescue her. Eventually he'll realize it's bullshit because there won't be a money trail—or a company. I also told him that I'm on vacation, spending time with you guys," he said, nodded at Mary Grace and Mercer, "until I head back to work. He invited me to see him in Miami."

"No way he's there." Skye took a bite of her pepperoni slice, unable to resist the smell any longer.

"You could call his bluff, tell him you want to see him in Miami," Brooks said quietly. She'd learned quickly that he was the quietest out of all of them. Made sense, since he used to be a sniper and they often went for long stretches without any human contact.

"I thought about that. But he's familiar with Miami. I don't think he's actually there, but he worked out of the Miami office for a decade. He'll have the upper hand. Not to mention all the CCTVs there. Skye's been careful with her appearance but I'd rather bait him somewhere where we control everything."

"What about the bioweapon?" Savage asked.

"What about it?" Colt's voice was tight as he stared hard at his friend.

Skye and Colt had given his friends most of the details of her disappearance, including her crime. It put her in a vulnerable position but if she was asking these people to shelter her, to help her potentially track down Gianni, she hadn't wanted to hold anything back.

He held up his hands in mock defense. "All he knows, or thinks, is that she died and the weapon was destroyed, right? Well, what if we put out feelers—as if they're from her—that she still has it and wants to sell it."

Colt shook his head. "He'll never believe she'd sell it."

"That's...not necessarily true," Skye said. "What if he thinks I'm desperate for money? If the price is low enough, I'll look desperate. And we won't give my identity away. Just let it be known there's a seller for it. A seller taking bids. He won't be able to resist. He wants to sell it himself. If he thinks he could get it for a steal..." She lifted a shoulder.

Colt didn't respond, just brooded and started eating. No one said anything and she wasn't shy about polishing off the rest of her food. That was one of the first lessons she'd learned in the field. Eat when you can because you never know when you'll get your next meal. In some cases that had proved to be very true.

* * *

"This is a nice neighborhood. Very respectable." Skye glanced at the one and two-story homes they drove past. They weren't cookie cutter, like in some subdivisions. The street lights were bright, illuminating the sidewalks and street. And it was very quiet, considering how late it was.

"Why do you sound surprised?" Colt's voice was dry as they headed down the road to his dad's home.

"Every time you talk about your dad, you have a tone. Like...I don't know. I guess I expected his house to look like the Death Star or something."

He barked out a laugh, which was what she'd intended. "He's a good man. But he can be difficult. We always butted heads."

So he'd said. Colt didn't talk about his father much, but she knew his mom had died not long after he'd hit adulthood. Cancer. His father and mother had apparently had a complicated relationship as well. Colt had lived in Redemption Harbor with his mother, and even though they'd never officially divorced, his parents hadn't lived together. Not truly. His father had worked in some sort of special division in the Corps—and been gone all the time, usually based in foreign countries. When he'd retired, he'd moved to Redemption Harbor a block from where Colt had grown up.

"I think he's part of a book club now," Colt muttered as he steered the truck they'd borrowed from Brooks into the driveway of a two-story Colonial-style home. The lawn was pristine.

"Seriously?"

He snorted. "No, not seriously. A gun club, maybe. He's in his fifties and still practices martial arts." As he turned off the engine, he rolled his shoulders once.

It was strange, seeing him so uneasy over a visit with his father. "We don't have to stay long."

"I know."

With her ball cap pulled low, Skye got out and met him at the front of the vehicle. His shoulders were stiff and his jaw tight. Immediately she took his hand in hers. "I've literally seen you face down the barrel of a loaded weapon without flinching."

He sighed and rolled his shoulders again. "Yeah, I know."

And that was all he said as they approached the front door. It swung open before Colt could knock and they came face to face with an older version of Colt. His dad was a little over six feet, lean but muscular like his son, and had dark hair peppered through with gray and bits of auburn.

"You have a beard now?" Colt blurted so suddenly Skye knew he hadn't meant to say it.

His dad half-smiled and ran a hand over it. "Yeah. Trying something new."

"It looks good," she said. "Makes you look distinguished. I'm Skye," She held out a hand, which he shook firmly, introducing himself as Senior—she knew his first name was also Colt.

Then he stepped back to let them in. "I was surprised when you called."

Colt let her walk in first, then shut the door behind them, his movements stiff and so out of character for the confident man she knew.

"We've got a problem," he said, motioning between him and Skye. "Related to work. Anyone from the Agency contacted you lately?"

"No."

Skye knew he had top-level clearance—or he had at one point—but he would have known what his son's job was regardless, since he would have been interviewed before Colt was hired.

"Are you cleaning guns?" she asked, knowing the question was a little weird, but not caring. She could smell the gun oil with a hint of citrus, and these two needed to talk about something they were both comfortable with so they could break through whatever this was. She might not have had the most conventional childhood—ha!—but she'd give anything to have her parents still alive.

Senior looked startled, but nodded.

"I love the smell of gun oil."

"You like weapons?"

She snorted. "That's like asking if Santa likes Christmas."

He smiled and motioned with his hand for them to follow. Skye ignored the annoyed look Colt gave her and followed the older man to a dining room where multiple weapons had been laid out on towels. Most were broken apart, in the process of being cleaned.

"Oooh, an M1911." She didn't touch it, but moved around the oval-shaped table to look at it. From 1911 to 1986 it had been the standard-issue sidearm for the armed forces. She had one herself and knew Colt did as well.

"It's how I got my name," Senior said.

She looked up from admiring the pristine weapon. "So...you were both named after Colt manufacturing, then?"

Colt gave a half-smile and nodded. "Yep. Grandpa named Senior after the manufacturer of his favorite sidearm."

"And I did the same," Senior said.

Somehow that seemed fitting, considering who these two men were. "You've been keeping secrets, Colt." He'd never told her that he was named after a weapon.

Colt just lifted an eyebrow, and okay, that was fair considering what she'd done.

"So what's going on? Are you in trouble?" his dad asked, crossing his arms over his chest.

"Things have gotten complicated." Colt rubbed a hand over the back of his neck.

"Your son and I used to be partners, so you know who I worked for." Okay they'd been way more than that, but calling him her boyfriend or lover felt too weird. "I faked my own death because someone threatened everyone in Colt's life. That was months ago. Now we think the man who threatened everyone Colt cares about—including you—might be on to the fact that I'm alive. Which means everyone who means anything to Colt is a target and needs to be careful." Maybe she should have let Colt tell his dad, but he seemed to be struggling with finding the words. This just got everything out into the open quickly. Like ripping a Band-Aid off. Now they could move forward.

"And Mary Grace is alive," Colt added. "Which has nothing to do with what Skye just told you. But you should know, we just rescued her from Mexico. For the time being we're hoping to keep it out of the media."

Senior blinked once, taking it all in stride Which wasn't really a surprise, considering he'd been in some type of special forces. "That's a lot of information to digest... I'm really glad to hear about Mary Grace. Now, who threatened you, son?"

"My recruiter."

Senior didn't even blink at that. "You need help bringing him down?"

"No...not yet anyway. We're working on something. I just wanted to let you know that you could come stay at Brooks's property if—"

"No one's running me out of my home. If someone wants to come at me, let them." He got the same stubborn look on his face Colt did when he'd made up his mind about something.

Before Colt could respond, she said, "If you want to get beat in a shooting competition, come out to Brooks's place, then."

"Beat by who?"

She smiled widely. "Me, of course. And I won't go easy on you either."

He tilted his head slightly, eyeing her curiously. "Long range?"

"Sounds good to me. But fair warning, I'm awesome."

"Is there enough room at your friend's place?" he asked Colt.

"More than enough."

"All right. Let me think on it. Anything else I need to know?"

"If you think you're being watched, contact me, but not over the phone. I don't know if your phones are being monitored. Feels unlikely, but just in case."

His father nodded once. "Okay. I'll grab a disposable cell from the store. I'll pay cash."

"Good."

"You guys hungry?"

"Ah, no, we already ate. Mercer made pizza."

Senior snorted. "I've been to one of his restaurants a few times. Good stuff."

For a few more minutes Skye stood by as Colt and his father engaged in awkward small talk. It was almost painful to watch, especially since she knew Colt wanted to basically demand his father come out to Brooks's property. Strained relationship or not, he needed his father to be safe. Especially if they were going to go after Gianni.

When things started winding down, Skye subtly took off her ball cap and dropped it onto one of the dining room chairs.

Senior walked the two of them out and once they were on the front porch, she turned to Colt. "Oh, I forgot my hat, will you grab it?"

He nodded before heading back inside.

Skye immediately spoke to Senior. "Look, Colt needs to be in the right headspace for going after this guy," she said quietly and quickly. "He won't come out and demand it, but he wants you at Brooks's place. If he knows you're safe, it'll be easier to do what needs to be done. And his well-being means more to me than anything."

Colt chose that moment to step back outside, her cap in hand. Senior didn't respond, not that she'd expected him to. Not in front of Colt.

So she smiled. "It was nice to meet you."

"You too." He gave her one of those half-smiles that were so much like Colt's. It was easy to see what he'd look like in a couple decades.

"Can I talk to you a second?" Senior nodded once at Colt, the question clear. He wanted privacy.

Skye took her cap and headed to the vehicle. Watching the two of them from the truck made her shake her head. They both stood stiffly, their facial expressions barely changing as they talked to each other. Then, one hard hand pump and they separated before Colt got into the driver's seat.

"So?" she asked once he'd pulled out into the street.

"So what?"

"What did he say?"

"He'll be coming to Brooks's tomorrow. He wants to pack up his stuff and feed his neighbors a lie about going on vacation in case someone comes sniffing around."

"Smart."

"Yeah. He also said I needed to put a ring on your finger." Colt shook his head slightly. "Said that you are utterly perfect for me."

She blinked, taken aback and definitely not sure how to respond, considering she'd been in Senior's company for all of ten minutes. "Oh."

"Really? Oh is all I get?" His voice was dry. "You can do better than that."

"Colt...I don't think now's the time to talk about...stuff."

"Stuff? Are you kidding me? I love you, Skye. And this is getting old."

"I love you too," she muttered.

"What was that?"

"Oh shut up, you big jackass! I love you too!" He was determined to make her say it. But saying the words, putting them out into the universe, made her feel raw and vulnerable. Because it made her even more afraid for him. For their future. Almost as if she was jinxing it.

When she'd faked her death, left him, she'd had to compartmentalize everything in her life, specifically her feelings for Colt. She'd never expected him, never expected everything he evoked inside her. Working for the CIA, helping strangers and risking her life on a constant basis had been easier than falling in love. She still felt like she was in a free fall when she was around him—or thought about him.

"I'm going to get that quote framed for our one year anniversary."

Gah. *One year anniversary?* What the hell was he doing to her? Nope. She could absolutely not go there. They needed to deal with Gianni, then…they could talk about other stuff. Oh yeah, she was going to avoid talking about this completely. "So what's the official plan once we get back to Brooks's?"

"You can't avoid talking about the future forever."

"I can for now…Come on."

He gave her a frustrated, sideways glance before turning back to the road. "Tonight I'm going to call one of my assets—using an alias Gianni doesn't know about. I'll tell him I've got a seller for a bioweapon who wants to move it fast. It'll get back to Gianni soon enough. A day, a week, he'll find out about it."

"Then he'll start hunting me."

"This time we'll be hunting him first."

She liked the idea of that a whole lot. But she didn't like the idea of Colt going after Gianni. She worried that he was too connected to the man. What if they went toe to toe and Colt flinched or paused and got himself killed?

Icy fingers danced down her spine at the thought. She'd done everything she could to keep him safe. No way was she going to lose him now.

CHAPTER SEVENTEEN

—Secrets.—

Seven months ago

Colt pushed up from the hotel bed when Skye walked out of the bathroom wearing nothing but a pair of panties—with the text *Congratulations—you made it this far* on the front. This woman constantly made him smile. Familiar hunger swelled inside him but there was something in her gaze, something distant he didn't like.

They'd arrived back in DC yesterday and opted to stay in a hotel room for a few days, wanting downtime and a little luxury after being in the jungle for the last couple weeks. Last night she'd gone for a workout in the hotel gym and when she'd come back, he'd felt the distance. As if she'd put up a wall between them.

"What's going on with you?" he asked as she picked up the robe she'd draped over the end of the bed and slipped it on.

She frowned at him as she pulled her damp hair from under the collar of the robe. "What are you talking about?"

"Are we good?" He pulled her close to him, wrapping his arms around her waist.

"Yeah. Of course." But that look was still there. The one that sent an arrow of panic through him. "I'm freaking exhausted, is all."

"We have been going hard the past few weeks." Holding her like this, feeling her body against his, his own body automatically reacted. Simply the way it was with her. If she started pulling away, he didn't know how to stop it. Didn't know if he could.

Sighing, she laid her cheek against his chest and just held him. "You think you'll do this forever? Our job?"

The question took him off guard. "Not field work, no." He loved what he did, but he wanted more from his life. If he and Skye ever did have kids—another thing that seemed to terrify her—he didn't want to be gone all the time. Even if they didn't have a family, he didn't want a life where he was constantly on the road. "Why? Feeling burned out?"

"A little, I think." There was a note in her voice that was slightly off and even though he wanted to fix whatever was going on, demand she open up, he knew that wasn't the way to go with Skye. If he tried that, she'd close up even more on him.

"I'm not married to this job," he said quietly.

She didn't say anything, just pulled back to look at him. Then she was on him, kissing him with an intensity that made him stumble back a step. He'd learned that if she didn't want to talk about something, sex was the way she communicated. It didn't take long before her robe and panties were tossed to the side, his own clothes joining them on the floor.

His cock was heavy between his legs, pressing against the flat plane of her abdomen as they fell onto the plush, king-sized bed.

Reaching between their bodies, she grasped his erection and started stroking him. He groaned into her mouth, his body on fire for her. He'd learned that there was nothing off-limits between them in the bedroom. He loved that about her.

Skye was giving and open with her needs, her wants—at least sexually. If she wanted him to go down on her, she told him. If he wasn't hitting the right spot, she told him that too. And she gave back everything she asked for, taking joy in everything she did. By now, however, he'd learned what made her tick, knew exactly how she liked to be kissed, teased, stroked.

Grasping her wrist, he pulled it away from him, even though he hated to lose her touch. Right now he wanted to make her crazy, to push her over the edge. Then do it all over again. If she thought she could put walls back up, pull away from him, it wasn't happening.

He guided both her hands above her head. "Stay put," he murmured against her mouth. The headboard was the tufted kind so he couldn't restrain her. This would have to do.

She arched her back as he began kissing down the column of her neck and bare chest. Outside lights from the busy city filtered in, illuminating her soft, bronze skin. When he reached the pale white line of an old scar under her ribcage, he brushed his lips over it, taking his time.

He did the same when he reached the even paler spider-web scar on the right side of her stomach. Her body was a warrior's.

His resilient and determined warrior, more beautiful to him because of the scars. And one day he'd learn all her secrets.

"How'd you get this one?" he murmured before gently raking his teeth over the scarring.

She speared her fingers through his hair and spread her legs wider. "Less talking."

"Tell me." He moved parallel from the scar until he reached her bellybutton.

She let out a light laugh as he teased it with his tongue.

"I'll torture you until you talk." He moved lower still, kissing over the smooth skin of her completely waxed mound. She always waxed before a mission—less maintenance, she said. Always so practical. He loved it either way.

"I like this brand of torture." Her voice was thick with desire.

He flicked his tongue over the pulsing bud of her clit once, twice...then stopped.

She dug her fingers into his head, but he moved higher, away from the pleasure point.

She huffed out an irritated breath. "Stray bullet hit me on a mission in Panama. Rescuing some diplomat's daughter. Now lick me," she demanded.

"Lick what?"

Growling in annoyance, she tried to move her legs together, as if to deny him, but he moved his hands between her inner thighs and held them firm. "You know what."

"I want to hear you say the word."

"You have a weird obsession with that word."

"Say it."

"Pussy. Lick my pussy." Her voice was raspy, her breathing coming out harsh now.

Oh yeah. He was working his woman up. Just the way he liked it. Dipping his head back down, he did exactly as she'd ordered and started teasing her slick folds until she was writhing against his face.

"So close." She dug her fingers into his scalp, not caring about his order to keep her hands above her head. Skye was like that, always doing whatever she wanted.

Something he loved about her. Then again, he loved everything about the woman. Most days he thought she was all in too. Until today. He'd sensed something off, and he wasn't sure what the hell was going on.

Her body was trembling, her breathing harsh and uneven. They'd done this enough that he knew she was close. He wrenched his head back. "Want to be inside you when you come." She spread her thighs to accommodate him and wrapped her legs around his hips as he thrust inside her. On a cry of pleasure, she arched her hips against his.

His balls pulled up tight as her inner walls tightened around him, clenching each time he thrust inside her. Every time he was with her, it was like coming home. Every. Single. Time.

He'd never thought it would be possible to feel this connected to someone. She knew everything about him and loved him anyway. Because he was no saint. But Skye didn't care.

Her fingers dug into his ass as she met him stroke for stroke. "I can never get enough of you." She said the words almost as an accusation.

He understood, because he felt the same way. Reaching between their bodies, he rubbed her clit as he crushed his mouth to hers. Over and over, he teased the little bundle of nerves until her inner walls convulsed around his cock, her orgasm slamming into her.

As soon as she let go, he did the same, releasing himself inside her, marking her, claiming her. The thought was primitive but he didn't care. He wanted to mark this woman, wanted to lock her down forever.

He'd even bought the ring.

Her head fell back as the remnants of her orgasm faded. All his muscles were pulled taut as he thrust one last time, his breathing erratic as he watched her slowly open her eyes.

She gave him a seductive smile that told him she was sated, relaxed. He loved seeing her like this. Their lives were so stressful and these moments between them far too few.

Though he hated to, he pulled out of her and rolled their bodies so that she was half splayed on top of him. Skin to skin. He rubbed a hand down her spine. "Want to order room service?" They'd planned to head out but he wouldn't mind staying in the rest of the night.

"Sounds good to me," she murmured.

Neither made a move to call. He didn't want to budge from this spot, and food would wait. He continued stroking his hand down her spine, savoring the quiet, intimate moment.

"You're the first person, other than my parents, I've ever told I loved." The quietly spoken words against his chest weren't exactly a shock. Not for the woman he knew. She'd never been in a serious relationship before him and her parents had been her only family—that she knew of, anyway. But he wasn't sure why she was telling him this now.

"You're the first woman I've ever told I loved." Something she should know, but he decided to spell it out. She was the last woman he would love. Telling Skye that, however, was likely to freak her out. Which was why he hadn't proposed yet.

He was waiting for the right time—if there was such a thing. He'd know the moment when it presented itself.

"Good." Her breath was warm against his chest. Then she lifted her head, pinning him with her pale blue eyes. "I...just want you to know that you're the best man I've ever known, Colt. Being your partner has been the best time of my life. I wouldn't trade this last year for anything."

It hadn't been quite a year, but he agreed. Except the tone of her voice also set off an alarm in his head. "You breaking up with me?"

She snorted softly and let her head fall back to his chest. "Shut up."

That didn't ease the dread gathering inside him. "That's not an answer."

She pinched his side. "No. I just wanted you to know. This time with you, I'll always treasure it."

That sounded a hell of a lot like goodbye. Or at least a warning that one was coming.

"I'm not going anywhere." He tightened his grip, pulling her closer. Her saying goodbye had to be bullshit. She might be complicated, but he knew how she felt about him. She couldn't hide that. Just like he couldn't hide his own feelings. He didn't want to. Not with Skye.

CHAPTER EIGHTEEN

—Everyone deserves one true friend.—

Colt and Skye stepped into the guest room Gage had turned into his temporary work station. Multiple computers were set up and he'd hung up a simple white board with pictures and names of interested buyers of the bioweapon. He'd been busy in the last twenty-four hours.

"Your dad settling in?" Gage asked without looking up from one of his monitors.

"Yeah. He's out with Brooks, helping fix some broken fences." Colt had been surprised his father had actually shown up but this morning right after breakfast, he'd arrived, bag in hand. And since his father couldn't sit still, Brooks had gladly put him to work.

"Good. All right, so far I've got six interested buyers."

"That's it?" Skye stepped forward, crossing her arms over her chest as she eyed the board.

"Well, six interested buyers who actually have the funds. We're making you look desperate but not so desperate you'll sell to just anyone."

Yeah, that had been something they both agreed on. Even if Skye was desperate she would still never sell to certain buyers on principle. Otherwise, Gianni might not believe this was her.

"Why no pictures for these two?" Colt motioned to the two names on the board without photos.

189

"Because I don't think they exist. This one," he said, pointing to the name Dae Jung, "has only existed on paper in the last two years. There's not even a passport linked to it. Not one I can find, anyway. It's linked to a shell corporation that, at the end of a very long electronic trail, leads back to China. And this one"—he tapped the empty space above the name Terrence Pace—"I think is your guy."

Colt straightened. "You think he's Gianni?"

"It's possible. The alias is good. I mean, really, really good. If I'd only peeled back the first few layers of his history, I wouldn't have suspected this was an alias. The driver's license on file looks similar to the picture you gave me of Gianni. But it's not him."

Colt only had one picture of Gianni—an eight-year-old photo from when he'd first been recruited. "You know who it is?"

"After reviewing the image I think it's a combination of different faces. Which means someone hacked the DMV and replaced the original picture with this image. Not too difficult if you have the skills. The image is a similar enough resemblance to Gianni that if he needed to use it, it would work fine, but it wouldn't trigger any facial recognition software. Which is the whole point for him. Maybe Pace isn't Gianni, but combined with what I've found so far trying to track him and this Pace being an interested buyer…there's a good chance it's your guy."

"Only way to know is if we get an in-person look at him." Skye's voice was grim.

"What other info do you have on him?" Colt asked.

Gage gave a rundown of the guy's holdings, financial accounts and addresses. His main one was listed in California. Which meant Colt would be planning a trip to the West Coast. This wasn't the kind of thing he could hire out. And he didn't want to alert anyone at the Agency. He was already on a short leash with his boss. Not to mention there was no telling if Gianni was working with anyone else. No, this had to be under the radar.

"I don't think you should go to California," Skye said, as if she'd read his mind.

"We need to see if it's him. If it is, we don't even need to set him up on a buy. If Pace is Gianni, I'll just take him out."

Her frown deepened. "You think he won't be protecting himself?"

"I won't know until I see for myself."

Skye had started to respond when Savage stepped into the room.

"I'll go," Savage said. "I was listening outside the door," he added when Colt frowned. "Even if Gianni knows my face he'll be less likely to look for me than you. If for some reason he's tracking your movements—and the fact that he recently called you is suspect—it makes more sense for an unknown like me to head out and track him."

"It might not even be him."

Savage shrugged. "Then we've lost nothing. I can go alone or bring Brooks with me. If all you want is recon, I'm your guy."

"Gianni is highly trained."

"So am I."

"I like it," Skye said. "He should go."

Colt glanced at her, surprised. She hadn't wanted anyone involved in this whole thing at all. Now she was siding with Savage?

She placed a hand on her hip. "Gianni freaking called you and you told him where you are. So far you haven't lied to him. If he's just testing the waters, seeing if you know anything about me, you've given him no reason to distrust you.

Unless of course he knows I'm alive, then this is all a moot point. But if he doesn't, then having Savage do recon is the smartest move. You know it too, you just want to go after Gianni yourself."

He clenched his jaw. Colt did want to go after Gianni, take him out and never worry about him again. Then they could figure out a way to bring Skye back to life without completely making their boss at the CIA lose his mind. He hadn't figured that part out yet. Right now, he was taking things one step at a time. And step one was to eliminate Gianni.

Colt hated that she was right. "Fine. You and Brooks both go. You can be each other's backup. And just get a picture or confirmation that Pace is Gianni. If he's not, come home. Hell, come home regardless. I want to bring him to us." It would be a hell of a lot easier to take Gianni out on Colt's own territory.

Savage nodded and gave a small grin. "We'll head out tonight. I've got my go bag ready."

"Thank you for doing this," Skye said. "I know it's for Colt, but still, thank you."

"I'm doing this for both of you." Savage left the room in a few long strides.

Colt scrubbed a hand over his face. Going after Gianni without the normal resources of the CIA was a pain in the ass, but Gage was damn good at what he did with computers. If he thought Pace might be Gianni, there was a good chance he was.

"Even if Pace isn't Gianni, at least we know that word's spread about the bioweapon." Skye leaned against the front of Gage's desk, arms still crossed over her chest as she stared at the board.

He didn't think she was really seeing it though. No, she was lost in her own head. He drank in the sight of her lean profile, the hard set of her jaw as she remained immobile. It wasn't often that she was still. Her auburn hair was down around her shoulders in soft waves rather than in her usual braid.

She made a frustrated sound and rubbed the back of her neck. When she turned and caught his gaze, she gave him a half-smile. The sight, like always, was a punch to his senses. The fact that she was alive, back in his life, and they were working together again... Yeah, he would be putting a ring on her finger soon. He didn't feel her pulling away from him anymore.

It was as if she'd embraced what was between them. Finally.

* * *

Three days later

"Dude will you stop? You're driving me nuts," Brooks said, not glancing at Zac. "Seriously, you're like a five-year-old."

"How are you not bored?" Zac realized how he sounded but stakeouts were mind-numbing. Still, he stopped throwing almonds at the side of Brooks's head.

"Maybe it's the stellar company." Brooks's voice was dry and he didn't look over from his binos.

They'd rented a boat tonight—their third day in California—and were staking out the residence of Terrence Pace from the ocean. The past couple days they'd tried other positions from around the property but there was no good visual. And if Pace was inside he hadn't come out yet. Not that they'd seen anyway. Jake Young, a guy who worked for a security company, had been coming and going, with groceries and other types of deliveries. But that was it. On almost three acres, the beachfront property had ultimate privacy from the front and from any neighbors. And if this Pace could afford this type of place, it was likely he could afford the bioweapon.

The water was the only way they might have a shot at actually seeing Pace. If they didn't see anyone tonight they'd be heading in tomorrow night.

That was a last resort though. They didn't want to risk being seen by anyone and tipping Gianni off that they were on to him—if Pace was even Gianni.

"This is why I could never do what Colt or Skye does," Zac said. Yeah, they saw a lot of action, but spies also spent a whole lot of time sitting on their thumbs just *waiting*. It was why spies trained so hard, working out like fiends. They had to stay in shape so when the situation went from zero to a hundred in seconds, they were ready.

His best friend snorted. "Yeah, that's the only reason."

"All right, I couldn't deal with all the politics." With his job, he ghosted into hard—aka impossible—to reach places and took care of business. Either with a weapon, or he simply retrieved things. He preferred stealing. Much cleaner and easier on his soul. Something he didn't want to think about right now.

"No shit. So, what's up with Leighton?"

Their friend had arrived at the ranch the day they'd left and he hadn't looked good. He'd lost at least ten pounds and there had been a haunted look in his eyes. "I don't know but he said he'd been thinking about taking a break."

"Yeah, he mentioned that a few months ago too." Brooks frowned, still not taking his gaze from his binos.

"Want me to take over?"

"Nah. I'll let you know when I'm ready. You thinking about quitting your job?" The question was abrupt, but Zac shouldn't be surprised Brooks asked.

Of all of his friends, Brooks knew him the best. He stretched his legs out and stared up at the spatter of stars. The moon was hidden, which was good for their purposes. The waves rolled softly, barely jostling the boat. "Maybe."

"I figured."

"What the hell would I do though?" A question he'd asked himself too many times to count. He was good at what he did, which probably wasn't something to be proud of. He'd thought about getting into personal security, but it would mean he worked for someone else and there would always be a boss to answer to. Yeah, he had one now, but there was a level of autonomy he liked.

"Start your own company. Join the RHPD. They're hiring. Come work on the ranch with me. Or—"

"It was rhetorical," he muttered, even if it hadn't been.

Brooks straightened suddenly, snapping Zac into work mode. Without asking if Brooks had seen something, he grabbed his own pair of Steiner tactical binoculars and raised them to his eyes. "Second story, second room from the left. Two French doors just opened," Brooks said.

Shifting over, Zac scanned to where Brooks had said and zoomed in on the man stepping outside. His heart rate kicked up a notch as he watched the man wearing a pullover sweater and lounge pants sit on a lounge chair, a drink in hand. His mouth was moving... Zac saw the earpiece and cell phone in his hand. Talking to someone.

"He does not look happy," Brooks murmured.

"No kidding." Thanks to the magnification he had a clear image of Mark Gianni's face.

"I'll call Colt." Brooks put his binos down but Zac kept his up, watching him.

"We could move in tonight, take him out." This was one kill Zac wouldn't feel guilty about. Mark Gianni had threatened Colt's family, friends, and caused serious pain to a man he considered a brother—making him think he lost the woman he loved. Not to mention Gianni wanted to buy a bioweapon that could kill hundreds of thousands—maybe millions—and sell it to the highest bidder. The world would be a better place without him.

Brooks didn't respond, just talked quietly into his cell phone. Zac zoomed out and panned over the rest of the back of the house—and spotted three guards. Well hidden, but three were in place...and another was patrolling. He hadn't seen them earlier and Brooks hadn't mentioned seeing any boots on the ground.

Putting the binos down, he moved to the cabin of the boat and started the engine, not bothering to tell Brooks what he was doing. It was time to get out of there. If Gianni or his guys spotted them, they might get suspicious. About half a mile down the coast, Brooks stepped up next to him at the wheel.

"Colt wants us to come home."

"Figured he would. I saw four guards."

"They must have come out when Gianni did."

"Yeah. And they've got to have video security." Probably sensors and other high tech stuff. Things that could definitely be manipulated, but without knowing the layout of the house, what system they were using, how many guards and how many security precautions were in place, it was stupid to attempt a takedown of Gianni. Not when it wasn't absolutely necessary. Zac figured that Gage would have no problem getting the architectural layout of the home, but it could set off a trigger if Gianni discovered someone was looking into his alias. Yeah, not worth the risk.

"At a minimum. We'll get him to come to us." There was a hard note in Brooks's voice, one Zac didn't hear often. Sometimes it was easy to forget Brooks had been a sniper. He seemed so laid-back—and normally he was. But when he was focused on something or someone, especially through his scope, watch out. "The plane ready for us?"

"On standby."

Good. They could get home and formulate a real plan for taking down this bastard. One that didn't involve Colt going off alone and half-cocked in an attempt to save them all. Hell no. Zac wasn't exactly surprised Colt had gone after Mary Grace without telling anyone, but that didn't mean he had to like it. And no way was he letting his friend take this on alone.

Not Colt and not his woman, Skye. Because she was just as bad as Colt. Faking her death instead of telling Colt what was going on? The kind of love that had taken, to sacrifice her career and life for Colt... He could respect that.

Other than for his friends and some of the guys he'd served with, he couldn't imagine making that kind of sacrifice for anyone. Especially not a woman. He was going to make damn sure Colt and Skye got a chance at a future.

CHAPTER NINETEEN

—Playing with fire.—

"**Y**ou ready for this?" Skye squeezed Colt's forearm, knowing this would be hard for him, even if he tried to deny it. They were going to set up his former mentor and yeah, Gianni was a piece of shit, but he'd been an important figure in Colt's life. The man had recruited him, changed the very course of his life. And maybe he hadn't been an actual father figure but he'd been pretty damn close.

"Yeah." He held his cell phone in his hand loosely but tension was visible in every line of his body.

"I can leave the room if you want." They were using the room that Gage had established as his work station so Colt could call Gianni and start the process of reeling the bastard in.

"No. I want you here. You deserve to be here." He took her hand in his.

"Let's do this, then. The faster we get it over with, the better." She wanted to get her life back. And there was only one way that would happen: when Gianni was behind bars. Or dead. She didn't much care which.

Nodding once, he pulled his hand from hers and made the call. "Mark, good to hear your voice." Disgust crossed Colt's face, but his tone was easy and believable. "Yeah...yeah. Listen, I have a problem..."

Gage tapped Skye on the shoulder and gave her a headset that was plugged into one of the laptops he was using to record this conversation. From this point forward they were recording everything so they could use it as evidence.

Giving him a grateful smile, she slid the headset on and got the full conversation.

"How could she be alive?" Gianni asked. The disbelief in his voice sounded real—and she figured it was.

"I don't know. It might not even be her, but an asset of mine has been hearing chatter about a bioweapon on the market. Very small pool of potential buyers. And the seller...it's a woman. One of Skye's old aliases. I can't believe it's her, but I have to find out and I don't know who else to turn to."

"Have you told the director?" Meaning Scott Hernandez.

"No. But there's something else I didn't tell you before. When I rescued my friend in Mexico, she'd already been technically rescued from the cartel's compound. Her rescuer was a woman—who wore a mask and revealed no personal details. This woman left Mary Grace somewhere safe with a way to call me. The Agency doesn't know but my friend told me. I think it might have been Skye."

They were slowly building up Gianni's trust, making it seem as if Colt was reluctant to admit this much to him. By now, if Gianni had been looking into Colt's recent rescue he might have heard about a mysterious woman who helped. So Colt had to give him the information, seem as if he was being transparent.

Gianni didn't respond so Colt continued. "If it is her, I don't want to burn her, but...I've got to find out for myself if this is Skye. If she faked her death she had to have had a good reason." The bit of desperation in his voice sounded damn believable. "I want to know why."

Gianni let out a long sigh. "I'll look into it, see what I can find out."

"That's not why I called. I have a meeting set up with the seller. I just don't have enough backup going in and I can't contact anyone at the Agency."

A long pause. "You want me to come with you?"

"I know I have no right to call you like this and ask such a huge favor, but I can't let this go. If it's her, I'm going to find out what the hell is going on. You're not with the Agency anymore so this won't be a conflict of interest for you—unless you make it one. If it is, just forget we ever had this conversation."

"Where's the setup for the meeting?"

"Uh uh. If you're in, I'll give you more details. You're the one who taught me never to trust anyone."

Gianni let out a short laugh. "That I did. Fine, I'm in. But what happens if it is her? What are you going to do?"

"Turn the weapon over to the Agency. Or destroy it."

"That doesn't answer my question. What are you going to do about her?"

"I...don't know." Any other answer would be a clear lie. Gianni knew Colt well enough to realize that he wouldn't turn on Skye. "I won't hurt her, and I won't turn her over to be arrested. You should know that going in."

"You're a fool, Colt. But I'll still help you. If she is selling a weapon, the only thing that matters is making sure it stays out of the wrong hands. What she does after we've gotten it doesn't matter. We can spin a story."

"So you're still in?"

"Yeah. You were right to call me. I've got a couple guys I can bring into this. How many do you have as backup?"

"Two."

"All right. I can bring in three more. Guys I trust to keep their mouths shut."

"How do you know them?"

"Private security. I won't read them in to the specifics. I'll just let them know I'm doing something that requires security."

"Send me their files. If I'm working with someone, I need to know who they are." The response by Colt was so standard to his way of thinking and behaving it would stay in character.

Skye was impressed by how well he was holding up having this conversation with Gianni. It had to be hurting him, but he never let on. Which just made her want to comfort him even more. And punch Gianni square in his face for causing Colt even an iota of pain.

"You'll have the files. Where's the meeting?"

"Hilton Head, South Carolina."

"Where?"

"Meet me there and you'll get the details. The meeting is tomorrow afternoon."

"Cutting it close."

"It's when the seller wanted it."

"I'll be able to fly out in the morning."

Skye listened as they ironed out details of where to meet. If it was up to Colt, he'd just put a bullet in Gianni's head when he saw him, but she'd convinced him they needed to bring the CIA into this. But only after they had Gianni on the hook. Now it appeared as if they did. From here it would be a matter of setting him up and getting him to confess to all of his crimes.

That would be the tricky part. Well, that and staying alive.

Colt shoved out a sigh of relief as he ended the call and set his cell phone down. "You get all that?"

"Yep," Gage said.

Skye slid her headset off. "You need to make another call."

He shook his head once, his expression resolute. "They could arrest you."

"I don't think they will." Skye had that worry too, but they needed to loop the CIA in on this. It was time. "They'll want to bring Gianni down once you tell them what he's done and what he's planning to do. Now we have the opportunity to prove that he set me up and that he's dirty."

"We should just kill him once he gets to Hilton Head. Destroying the body will be easy enough."

"If we do that we lose the chance to prove his guilt. Then I might never get my life back." Now that she could see it in the distance, she wanted it. She wanted a future with Colt so badly she could taste it. This was what happened when you let people into your life, when you started to care.

"If they arrest you, I'm breaking you out of prison," he finally said.

Her heart warmed at his words, and she had no doubt they were true. "I would expect nothing less."

Sighing, he rubbed a hand over the back of his neck, that familiar action making her smile. Then he made the call she'd been waiting for. "Director Hernandez... We need to talk."

* * *

Using his stolen credentials, Mark hacked into the CIA's database again, searching for anything Colt might be linked to. When he didn't find anything, he started making phone calls.

And came up with nothing that indicated Colt had been lying to him.

It wasn't hard to believe Colt would go after Skye if he thought she was alive. Though Mark was pissed that she'd managed to fool him. That setup had been perfect—not that he would expect less from her. She'd been trained well.

He couldn't imagine Skye selling a bioweapon, however. That...didn't sit well with him. The only way he could imagine her doing it was if she needed money to get out of the country.

Using the house's intercom system, he buzzed Jake Young. "My office, now."

A few minutes later, Young stepped inside. The man worked for a well-known security company. Most of the men and women who worked there were former military and all were well-trained. Mark knew the owner personally—under his Terrence Pace alias. He'd also been specific in his requirements when he hired security guys. He didn't want Boy Scouts on his payroll.

"I need five guys for a job. I'm going to be meeting with someone about a complicated purchase." For the most part the guys he'd hired as security didn't ask questions. Of course he hadn't done anything to raise suspicion. He was just a wealthy businessman to them; one who required security. "It will be out of state and we'll be leaving as soon as possible."

"Okay."

"There will be weapons at this meeting."

Young shifted slightly. "My men will be armed. What kind of meeting is this, and who will be there?"

"Someone is selling something valuable. The seller will have armed guards." That was all he was willing to give up. Even if he'd specifically hired guys who were supposed to keep their mouths shut, he was trusting no one with this information. "Money and product will change hands. It should be simple, but just in case they try to screw me over, I need backup." Young was silent for a long moment so Mark continued. "It's not people, drugs or weapons being sold." Which left a lot out there, but the most obvious assumption would be art or antiquities and Mark didn't think this guy would care about any of that. He knew the company's reputation—which was why Mark had hired them.

"Okay. We won't do anything illegal, but my men and I will act as your security."

"Excellent. There is one more thing. An associate of mine has set up this meeting. He has a connection to the seller. One that might disrupt the buy and result in people getting injured. That's the last thing I want. I will need your men to restrain him—but not hurt him. I just want him restrained until the meeting is over. He'll be angry but it will ensure no one is injured, and everyone walks away happy." Before Young could respond, Mark continued. "There's a twenty-five thousand dollar bonus to you and your men—for each of you—who take this job."

Young nodded once. "I'll get my guys together. Are we flying private or commercial?"

"Private." He didn't want Mark Gianni or Terrence Pace to show up on any flight manifest. Luckily he knew a way around that.

CHAPTER TWENTY

—FUBARed.—

This was it. Mark steered into the driveway of a boarded-up three-story home that must have been hit by the recent hurricane. The entire strip of road for the past mile and a half had shown nothing but either washed-away houses or boarded-up ones likely damaged by flooding. He could see where the waterline had been on this house, right at the top of the first floor. Colt leaned against the front door of the place.

"This is my guy," he said to Young as he put the SUV in park. "Stay here until I tell you otherwise." Exiting the vehicle, he nodded at Colt, who came forward, his strides even.

"Those your guys?"

That was just like Colt, not bothering with small talk. "Yeah."

"You trust them?"

He lifted a shoulder. "As much as anyone."

"Good enough."

"So where's this meeting?" Colt hadn't told him anything, much to his frustration. Just that the meet would take place in Hilton Head. Then he'd given him this address. He also wanted to know where Colt's men were. Making sure they were neutralized was something he had to deal with as well.

"End of this road. There's a house right on the end of the peninsula. There's a boat idling on the water. The seller...it's Skye."

"You've talked to her?" Shit. This could very well be a setup by Colt if he knew what Mark had done.

"No. Set up some recon yesterday. Saw her on one of my video streams going into the place. Didn't plan on the seller coming in from the water so the recording is at an odd angle, but it's her. She arrived an hour ago. Our meet is supposed to be in ten minutes."

"How many people are with her?" Mark asked.

Colt's body language was contained, but Mark could see the frustration in his expression. He was pissed about Skye lying to him. And he could never find out why she'd faked her death.

"Just two. Unknowns. I've never seen them before."

Mark glanced around, looking for Colt's own people. "Where are the guys you said you're bringing?"

He shook his head. "I've got them sitting tight for me. I...just want to see her. I think it's better if only I talk to her. Whatever she's doing, I think I can talk her down from it. This isn't the Skye I know and if I go in with a bunch of people, shit will go bad. I know what I said—"

Mark struck out with his military-grade Taser. Colt's eyes widened and he went to block him, but he was too slow. As soon as it made contact with Colt's neck, he crumpled to the ground.

Behind him, Mark heard one of the doors open. "He's not to be hurt. This is the guy I told you about. I just want him restrained while I take care of this."

It was clear Young didn't like it, but he nodded and slapped flexi-cuffs on Colt's wrists before hauling his limp body up. A twenty-five thousand dollar bonus for an hour's worth of work would make anyone bend the rules.

Mark helped carry him to the back of the SUV where they deposited him. He took a quick photograph of Colt tied up and unconscious. "The meeting is at the end of this road. You guys stay here. I'm going in alone."

"Sir—"

He shook his head. Now that he knew Skye only had two guys with her and that Colt's own people weren't here, he was going to see her right now. He could easily take on three people and get what he'd come for. No matter what, Skye was going to be dead by the end of the day and the bioweapon would be his.

* * *

Skye hated everything about this plan, but this was the way it had to be. It was the only way they could get Gianni for all his crimes. There was no way he could talk himself out of this situation. Of course, that was only if things went according to plan.

And how often did things go pear-shaped in the field? *Ugh.* She was terrified something would happen to Colt. During past operations with him she'd always had a healthy dose of fear for him, but this was different.

The man they were up against was smart, calculating, and he knew both of them. It stood to reason he might figure out their intent. They'd pretty much given him this golden opportunity to attack, and if he thought hard enough about it, he might realize this was a setup.

"Gianni's here," Gage said through her earpiece. "And he's alone." Gage, along with a team of FBI agents—who'd been called in by Director Hernandez—were in one of the boarded-up homes, watching and waiting. There were a couple CIA agents too, but this wasn't foreign soil so the FBI was taking lead. Something she hated. She didn't know any of them, didn't know how capable they were. Yeah, they had training but they weren't *her* people.

"How's Colt?" she asked Gage. Bringing him in on this op had been her only stipulation. She and Colt had both agreed to do this only if Gage was part of the team. They needed someone they trusted working with them.

"Knocked out, but he's fine. Once Gianni is inside with you, the team will send guys to pick him up."

She didn't want to wait; she wanted them to get him right freaking now. But she held her tongue.

"He's approaching the stairs." The stairs Gage referred to led to the first level of the house, which was up on stilts.

Her heart rate increased at the thought of coming face to face with Gianni again. The man who'd ruined her life. She wanted to bash his face in, but that would have to wait. Maybe forever. Because this wasn't just about her. This was about Colt and his friends, who'd stuck their necks out for her, trying to help her get her life back. And it was about the two FBI agents in the room with her posing as her bodyguards.

"You ready?" she asked Ben Sanchez, the agent closest to her. A Hispanic man about five feet ten and solidly built, tattoos ran up and down his exposed arms. She knew they were temporary but they looked real. And he looked the farthest thing from any type of agent. He had the thug look down pat.

He didn't move from his spot next to the heavy oak table— thoroughly water damaged and molding on the legs—that held the fake bioweapon. "We got this. You just need to get him to confess."

Yeah, easy peasy. "No problem," she muttered.

"At the front door," Gage said.

They had cameras all over the place, the tiny invisible ones Gianni wouldn't be able to see. He was letting his greed, and his trust in Colt, blind him to this setup. Which was good and bad. Because once he realized he'd been had, his reaction would not be good.

A loud bang sounded from the front door. "Open the door, Skye! I know you're in there."

She froze for a second, surprised he wasn't being subtle.

"Open it," she said to Camila Sanchez—no relation to Ben—the other agent, a Hispanic woman about her size and height.

Camila strode to the door, looking nothing like an agent either, and everything like a badass biker chick. The Feds had chosen these two agents because they were so new to the bureau and it was highly unlikely Gianni would know them. A few moments later Camila strode into the room, her weapon right at Gianni's temple, holding it like a pro.

"I checked him, he's clean," Camila said.

Skye's heart rate increased again as she met Gianni's gaze. He looked just as she remembered. Not quite six feet, with blond hair, brown eyes and a forgettable face. He was everyman, able to blend in anywhere. Wearing a suit and dress shirt, no tie, he looked perfectly at ease. There was a reason he'd been so good at his job.

Keeping her voice as cold as she knew her eyes were, she said, "Give me one good reason I shouldn't kill you right now."

"In my front pocket, pull out my cell phone." His expression was neutral. Even with a pistol at his temple. Smug, too. God she hated the man.

Keep your cool, she ordered herself. *Do not attack him.* She simply nodded once at Camila, who pulled the cell phone out.

"Code six-nine-two-five will open it. Look at the first picture."

Skye held out her hand, took the phone and did as he said. When she saw Colt tied up and unconscious she slammed the phone down to the ground. "What the hell have you done to him?" Even if she knew Colt was okay, she didn't have to fake her reaction much. Seeing him like that pissed her off.

"He's fine. And you'll be fine too if you give me what I want."

"You ruined my life. I'm not giving you shit."

"You will do exactly what I want."

Skye's gaze narrowed. "You'd really kill him? He trusts you. You're his friend, his mentor."

He didn't respond, just watched her, as if he was carefully choosing his words.

"How'd you find me?" she asked when he didn't answer.

"Chatter. And…word is that you're selling something you stole a while ago."

"Because of you."

No response. Damn him.

"You know what? Fuck you." Skye nodded at Camila and started to pick up the metal case on the table. "Shoot him and let's go. We'll be able to sell this to someone else."

"If you kill me, Colt's dead."

She stopped, her hand on the handle. "At this point I don't know that I actually care. I've been on the run for months because of you. Living in shitty motels and trying to lie low. It sounded noble at the time, sacrificing myself for him, but I'm done with being a martyr. I'm getting the hell out of the country, and thanks to you I've got the perfect way to make enough money to do it."

"If I don't make a call in five minutes, Colt is dead."

She lifted a shoulder. Even though she hadn't heard that Colt was okay, she had to believe in the team, believe that they'd been able to rescue him. "So what? You'll be dead too. Which means my problems are over." He paused and for a moment, she saw a brief flicker of panic enter his gaze. *Good.* She wanted him afraid. Wanted him to know what it felt like. "I'll pay you double what you're asking. And I'll pay in clean diamonds. No wire transfer, no electronic trail. Easy for everyone."

She paused, as if contemplating it. And she wasn't surprised when Ben and Camila exchanged a look, as if this sounded good to them as well. They were damn good actors.

"Colt's safe and Gianni's guys are in custody." Gage's voice came through her earpiece, his words the only thing she truly cared about. Colt was safe.

Relief swelled inside her but she had to shove her emotions, her reaction back down and keep all her focus on the monster in front of her. With a new shot of confidence, Skye shook her head at Gianni. "We're not going to another location so you can rip us off and kill us. No, we'll take our chances with another buyer."

"I've got clean diamonds on me. Tell your girl not to get trigger happy." Slowly, he lifted his shirt to reveal a tactical vest. He pulled on something and she heard Velcro tearing apart as a small pouch separated. "A quarter of the gems are here. I'll give this to you as a good faith payment—and so you can have them verified. You get the rest when we meet in a neutral, public location. One where no one gets trigger happy and we all walk away happy."

Skye eyed the diamonds, annoyed that the FBI agent hadn't felt the pouch when she'd checked him. That was rookie shit. "You already screwed me over once."

"I did you a favor."

You bastard. "How do you figure that?"

"You and Colt were never going to work out. You made him weak—and vice versa. I've seen your file. You're skilled. Obviously. You managed to fake your death and stay dead with no one the wiser. Now you can start over with a lot of money, live the life you want with no constraints. No rules from the Agency."

"Is that why you're doing this? No more rules or constraints? Colt always said you were married to the job, that you were a patriot." She snorted. "You sure had him fooled."

Gianni's jaw tensed. "I *believed* in everything I did—until they left my partner to die. He gave up everything for the job. They can all rot in hell. We doing this or not?"

She nodded slowly and tightened the pouch, scooping the gems up. "What are you going to do with the bioweapon?"

"Why the hell do you care?"

"I'm curious."

"Sell it to someone else—a country who will pay very good money for this type of weapon. Someone you don't have the balls to sell it to." The derision, the complete loathing of her came through in his words and expression.

And that was all she needed to hear, because she'd done it. Got him to hang himself with his own words. Hell, she didn't even have to signal anyone. The Feds would move in now. They wanted to scoop up Gianni now, to question him and find out who else he was working with, if anyone.

She hated him, hated this whole situation, but if it got Gianni locked up and Colt was safe, she could deal with this less than ideal ending. In an ideal world he'd be six feet under, but she could settle with getting her life back. "I'll give you a number to contact me. We'll set up a meeting tomorrow. As soon as these are verified."

He nodded—and the world around them exploded in noise. Her ears rang as a bang and flash of light exploded from Gianni's pouch.

Sonofabitch. Skye stumbled, automatically reaching for her holstered weapon as stars flashed in front of her eyes.

"Breaching now!" Gage shouted into her earpiece, the sound over pronounced as her ears rang.

Even though she could barely see, she ducked down behind the table, trying to find some sort of cover. White stars flickered in her vision, her head fuzzy as she tried to crawl toward the kitchen area. The male agent was in front of her, doing the same.

Pop. Pop. The distinctive sound of small arms fire.

Shit.

Dirt and debris crunched under her hands as she swayed while she crawled. Gianni had released a flash bang—one that should have been discovered in his body search. Either the female agent had made a rookie mistake or she was in league with Gianni. Skye was betting on the former.

Bang. The door slammed open from the front of the house. Backup had arrived. The stars were starting to clear from her sight—as a heavy, muscled arm wrapped around her neck.

"You stupid bitch," Gianni snarled, yanking her to her feet.

She gasped as her airway cut off, stumbling as he pulled her back flush to his chest. Her vision was clear as she felt the muzzle of a gun press to her temple.

Ah, hell.

She didn't want to die. There were so many damn things she wanted to do. To say to Colt. But an icy calm slid through her veins as she stared out at the scene in front of her.

The female agent was on the ground, blood pooling around her middle. Her chest was rising and falling. Oh hell. Three men dressed in full battle gear were fanned out in front of her. They all wore ballistic helmets and plate carriers and held M4s—all pointed at her and Gianni.

"Drop your weapons or she gets a bullet in the head." His voice was surprisingly calm, but she could feel the tremor in his hand as he held the pistol to her head.

She wasn't going to get out of this alive. But neither would he. Her only solace. She hated that she'd never get to tell Colt how much she truly loved him. Not some half-ass admission either. She also hated that he would mourn her again, have to suffer because she'd died. Man she hated Mark Gianni. "You're going to die here," she rasped out. Her throat was raw, sore and he wasn't letting up on his hold.

"Shut up and drop your weapon," he snarled.

She still clutched the pistol she'd pulled out earlier. And screw him. She wasn't letting it go. She couldn't twist enough to shoot him—not unless she shot through herself first. "Just shoot me now. Then they'll fill you full of bullets. I might not want to die, but knowing that you'll go down too... Shoot me, you pathetic coward. Shoot me and make the world a much better place."

"Colt was in on this," he snarled in her ear.

"Obviously, you dumbass. He fed you exactly what you wanted to hear."

His grip tightened and she tensed, bracing for what she knew was coming—when his hold suddenly loosened. *What. The. Hell.*

"I'm putting my weapon down. I'm disarming myself now." Gianni's words were calm, smug. As he slowly lowered the weapon, she swiveled, pointing her own directly at his head.

She heard the clatter of his weapon hitting the floor as he slowly raised his arms. The satisfied glint in his eyes made all the hair on her arms stand up. What the hell was going on?

"They'll never lock me up," he murmured. "I know too much. Have too much to give them. You think I wasn't ready for this possibility? I'll end up in a cushy safe house—and you'll never be safe from me," he whispered.

She smashed her pistol across his face as two of the agents took over, twisting him and slamming him to the ground as they cuffed him. He'd just shot one of their own, so they wouldn't go easy on him. But they also wouldn't kill him. Even if it was what he deserved.

Stepping back, she turned and ran right into Ben. "How's Camila?" she asked.

"Shot. Twice. Both missed her vest. One shoulder and another lower abdomen. She's being loaded up for transport to the nearest hospital now," he said as he made his way to the front door.

Skye fell in step with him as more armed Feds moved in. Her part was done and she needed to see Colt. She'd check up on the agent later.

"You still with me, Gage?" she asked quietly.

"Yeah. Your boy is foaming at the mouth and about to start punching Feds to see you. Better get your ass outside."

Her heart rate went into triple time as she burst out of the house and into the sunlight. It took her only a few seconds to see Colt standing next to a man wearing an FBI windbreaker. His arms were crossed over his broad chest, his jaw tight—until he saw her.

She wasn't aware of moving, of sidestepping every single person in sight until she had her arms around his neck and his were locked around her. "I knew it was part of the plan, but when I saw you in that trunk, bound and unconscious..." She buried her face in his neck and inhaled deeply. "I'm sorry for what I did all those months ago. Maybe I could have found another way."

His grip tightened. "Stop. You did what was right."

She pulled back to look at him, but kept her arms around him. "I know it hurt you though. And if I thought you were dead...it would have destroyed me. I should have found a way to let you know. God, Colt, I'm so damn sorry for all the pain I caused you. And I'm sorry I'm such a coward about saying the L word. I love you so much it terrifies me. And I'm going to tell you every damn day. I love you."

He shook his head, searching her gaze with his. "Stop. No more apologies. I wasn't in your shoes. Marry me, Skye. Not next year or in a few months, but as soon as possible." His voice cracked slightly and she was pretty sure that was a sheen of wetness in his eyes. "I don't have it with me, but I have a ring. So this isn't some spur-of-the-moment proposal. Marry—"

"Yes." She didn't even have to think about it and he didn't need to ask twice. She threaded her fingers through his dark hair as she looked up at him, cupping the back of his head. There was a shitload of stuff they needed to figure out and a ton of paperwork and other crap they'd have to wade through. Especially her, since she'd faked her death. But none of it mattered. Only Colt did, and she could hardly believe that she had a chance at a life with him now.

The smile he gave her was so real, so disarming, it slammed through her entire body. There was a raw vulnerability there she'd never seen. He looked...happy. And she felt the same. No matter what, she knew their life would never be dull.

He leaned down, starting to kiss her, then he froze, his gaze snapping past her. She turned in his arms and stiffened when she saw two Feds in tactical gear frog-marching Gianni down the stairs.

The bastard spotted them immediately and still had that smug look on his face. She seriously, seriously wanted to wipe it off. Her hands balled into fists and she'd taken a step toward him when Colt launched forward like a torpedo.

She started to go after him, but knew he needed to do this. If he wanted to talk to Gianni, or maybe break his jaw, then she wasn't going to interfere.

Moving like the lethal predator he was, Colt stalked up to Gianni and the two agents. One of the men held out a hand, as if to stop Colt. Skye stepped forward, but Colt raised his palms in a surrendering motion. Whatever he said seemed to appease the agent.

Both the armed guys took one step back as Colt leaned in to say something to Gianni. Gianni laughed in his face and said something back—and then Colt did exactly what she'd thought he'd do.

Moving lightning quick, he hauled his fist back and slammed it right into Gianni's nose. Blood spurted everywhere as his head snapped back.

One of the agents lunged at Colt, shoving him back as the other man hoisted up Gianni's now limp body. Colt shrugged the guy off and headed back to her, uncaring about anyone else.

Skye took her earpiece out as he reached her, loving him more than ever. "You ready to get the hell out of here?"

He nodded and slid his hand in hers. Feds were everywhere and she knew they'd have to head down to the local office to fill out paperwork, but there was no reason they couldn't drive alone.

They stepped up to the back of the command center van, which must have moved in as soon as Gianni had gone inside the house.

Colt knocked on the back door and she wasn't surprised when Gage opened it. "You ready to go?"

Gage nodded as Skye handed him her earpiece. He set it down on one of the work centers and jumped from the back of the van.

"Where are you guys going?"

Skye turned at the sound of Director Hernandez's voice. Wearing a nondescript black windbreaker—no FBI one for him—and aviator sunglasses, he looked as he always did. Calm and collected.

"The Feds have this under control," Colt said. "We're going to drive to the local office, meet the head agent there and fill out paperwork. Unless you want us to stay?"

Hernandez just stared at Colt before his gaze slid over to Skye. She couldn't see his eyes because of the sunglasses but she didn't need to. He was beyond pissed at her. He thought she should have handled things differently, should have come to him. Maybe he wasn't wrong. Hindsight was a bitch though. The only reason he wasn't hanging her out to dry was because she'd assisted in bringing Gianni down and because she, and her parents, had given a lot to this country. He'd flat out told her as much before this op.

"I'll meet you all there soon," he snapped before turning away and jumping into the back of the mobile command center.

It didn't take her, Colt and Gage long to find an unoccupied SUV to borrow. Once the three of them were inside, she finally let out a breath of relief. "I'm surprised you didn't kill Gianni with that punch," she murmured.

Colt snorted and gave her the strangest look. One she couldn't begin to decipher.

"We going to pick up the others?" Gage asked from the back seat.

"No, but Savage texted me. He and Brooks are going to meet the others back at the hotel. We'll go to them once we're done with the paperwork."

Every one of Colt's friends had made the drive to Hilton Head—which really wasn't that far from Redemption Harbor—and had been moral support while Skye and Colt dealt with Gianni. Though to be fair, Brooks and Savage had been more than moral support.

Brooks had set up with a scope from one of the nearby unoccupied houses, watching Colt and Gianni's meeting point. If Gianni had pulled out a gun instead of a Taser, he'd be dead right now. Knowing Colt had that kind of backup had been the only reason Skye had been okay with this operation. Because she only trusted the Feds so far.

"Who were the security guys with Gianni? And where are they?" she asked. Gianni had sent Colt a file on the men he'd be bringing, when he hadn't thought this was a setup. The guys had looked clean on paper, but she'd assumed he'd sent bogus information.

"Just hired guys. They had no idea what was going on. He gave them a bullshit story about why he'd tased me. None of them have criminal records. They were taken in for questioning and they'll probably be charged with a few misdemeanors—maybe lose their jobs—but the Feds don't give a shit about them."

Leaning back against the headrest, she sighed. "Gianni looked so smug. He told me he was going to give them information so good they'd set him up in a safe house and he'd never see a day of prison."

"He'll be dead within three days." Colt's voice was ice-cold and he sounded certain of that fact.

Gage went still in the back seat. Skye didn't respond or ask questions. If Colt was sure, there was a reason. And she wasn't going to ask any questions now. Not in an FBI-owned vehicle. It was doubtful the thing was bugged, but this wasn't the kind of conversation to have here. So she would wait.

Instead of responding, she reached across the center console and took Colt's hand in hers, linking their fingers together. This was finally over. They could finally start their lives together.

CHAPTER TWENTY-ONE

—She's worth it.—

Three days later

Colt braced himself as he knocked on his boss's door. Time to face the music.

"Come in," Hernandez called out.

Stepping inside, Colt quickly scanned the room. Looked as it always had. Awards hung on the pale gray walls, but there was no actual art. A big desk, two bookshelves and a filing cabinet took up the rest of the space.

"Sit," Hernandez ordered, not bothering to get up.

Colt sat, ready for whatever was to come. He'd made his choice, made a hard decision he knew would have ramifications. And he was willing to take the consequences. If he hadn't been, he'd have been long gone and off the grid by now.

"Mark Gianni died last night." Hernandez watched him carefully.

Colt didn't even bother trying to look surprised. Hernandez would see right through it. "If you're waiting for tears, there won't be any." His voice was dry.

"Ricin poisoning. You know anything about that?" His boss lifted a dark eyebrow.

"Should I?"

Hernandez didn't respond, just sighed and looked over at his wall of awards. "You're a good agent, Colt."

Okay so this wasn't going as he'd expected. He actually hadn't expected this meeting at all; he'd thought men in suits would show up at his place and arrest him for murder. You never knew with the Agency.

"But Skye Arévalo will always be a problem for you. She was a good agent too. But she didn't follow protocol and because of that, things could have gone a lot differently." He looked at Colt then, his brown eyes hard. "My bosses are letting her actions go because of the part she played in bringing down a dirty agent. And because we don't need the media attention. All of this will be swept under the rug. But you can't be with her. You can't have a relationship with her. It will destroy your career."

There was no way he was leaving Skye, no matter what happened. "I still have a career?"

Hernandez nodded once. "You've done a lot for us over the years."

"So has Skye."

He nodded again. "I won't deny that. Because of her service—and all her parents' sacrifices—we can't hang her out to dry. There would be too much of an uproar at the Agency."

Ah, the real reason they weren't going after her. Because Skye was a legend and her parents had stars on the wall. That, combined with the fact that they didn't want to face media scrutiny, not after the shitstorm the last director had faced, made sense.

"But you can't be with her. I need to know you understand that. If you want a shot at having my seat, at being a director yourself one day, you have to distance yourself from her."

"I understand." At his words, Hernandez sighed. But Colt stood. "You'll have my resignation letter in your inbox by the end of the day."

"Colt—"

"No. I'm not making this decision lightly. I've already got the letter typed up. I'm out." Unless of course Hernandez decided to arrest him for killing Gianni. Which Colt had. They'd have a tough time proving it, considering how many people had been in contact with Gianni since his arrest. Not to mention the man had shot an FBI agent. That gave Gianni a lot of immediate enemies. All well trained. They'd be hard-pressed to prove Colt had injected him when he'd thrown that punch. No one wanted all the media scrutiny a case like this would bring. It was his only saving grace.

Sighing, Hernandez nodded and stood. "I'll need your credentials."

Colt emptied his pockets, handing everything over to his now former boss. In the last couple days he'd been privy to all the details of Mark Gianni's life over the last year. He'd helped rip apart his former mentor's life and they'd discovered that thankfully he'd been working alone in his attempt to sell the bioweapon. All for greed. Sure, Gianni could blame it on his deceased partner being left out in the wind, but the truth was, he'd let his own greed and ego blind him.

"What are you going to do now?" Hernandez asked.

"I have no idea." Not exactly true. He planned to marry the woman he loved as soon as humanly possible. But he didn't think throwing that in Hernandez's face was such a good idea.

His boss was letting him walk on Gianni's murder. Colt was going to take the win and get the hell out of here and back to his woman, his future.

CHAPTER TWENTY-TWO

—Every end is a new beginning.—

"What is this place?" Skye eyed the huge warehouse Colt had parked in front of on one of the harbors in Redemption Harbor. The place was quiet, if a little rundown. The grass surrounding the building hadn't been cut in ages and she didn't see a sign signaling what this place was.

"It's mine. I put in a cash offer and it's been accepted. Just have to sign the contract after an inspection." Colt opened his door and got out so she followed suit, beyond intrigued. He'd arrived back from DC yesterday and had been quiet about how the meeting with his boss had gone.

For once she'd decided not to push. The only question she'd had was whether he would be arrested for murdering Gianni. He'd gone behind her back, behind everyone's backs, and made the decision to take Gianni out no matter what. When Colt punched him, he'd also injected Gianni with ricin. Toxic, deadly, with no known cure. Simple and effective.

She wasn't angry. Yes, she wished he'd come to her about it, but she understood why he'd done it. To protect them. All of them. Mark Gianni would never be a threat to her, his friends, family or him again.

"Is this your new home? Because honestly, it's a little better than that sad condo you've got back in DC." She joined him at the front of the truck, leaned against the hood. Once he'd returned to Redemption Harbor last night all they'd done was have sex. She couldn't imagine when he'd even had time to put in an offer on this place.

When he turned to her, his expression was serious and the bottom of her stomach dropped out. "I quit my job and put the condo on the market."

She blinked.

"And it appears as if Hernandez is letting everything go with Gianni. They got enough information from him before he died... And they don't want a media circus. Arresting one of their own for killing one of their own? Yeah, not happening."

The relief that slid through her was potent. If he'd been arrested, she'd have broken him out of prison and fled the country with him, but to know he was able to walk away... She was damn grateful. "But why'd you quit? You love your job."

"No. I love helping people. And we'll never know if they'd have cut a deal with Gianni, but I think they would have. He'd have never seen the inside of a prison cell and none of us would have been safe. Not truly. I have no regrets but I'm done with the Agency."

She didn't know whether to be shocked or relieved. Maybe she was a bit of both. "They told you to stay away from me, didn't they?" Hernandez had agreed to help her "resurrection," spinning some story about how she'd been deep undercover. It had been a pain in the ass to get all her paperwork filled out but it was a small price to pay. Hernandez had been pissed at her though; had told her in no uncertain terms that she was *persona non grata.* Which was fine with her. She'd only been concerned about Colt's career. She couldn't believe he'd quit.

Colt didn't respond. But she had her answer. Of course Hernandez had told Colt to stay away from her. She should have seen that coming.

Instead of answering, Colt went down on one knee and pulled out a small box.

Her heart skipped a beat as he opened it to reveal a platinum band with an engraving on it. The infinity symbol. He might have asked her to marry him already, but things had been crazy since the day of Gianni's arrest and they hadn't talked about his proposal since.

"I already have your answer. Now I want you to wear my ring." He pulled it out and slid the simple band onto her left ring finger.

Holding her hand out, she smiled at the sight of it, liked the feeling of being claimed by him. "No diamond?"

"I knew you'd hate it," he murmured, standing up and pulling her into his arms.

Another smile tugged at her lips and she laughed. He really did know her. A diamond would catch on things and get in the way, but this was perfect. Beyond perfect. "I love you so much, Colt Stuart."

"And I love you, Skye Arévalo." He brushed his lips over hers, deepening the kiss until he had her pinned against the truck. Heat flooded her body, pouring out to all her nerve endings.

She didn't care if they were outside, she was going to feel him inside her in the next sixty seconds. There was no one else around this area and the warehouse blocked any potential boaters on the nearby harbor. She'd hoisted up, wrapping her legs around his waist, when she heard the sound of gravel crunching under tires.

"Hell," he murmured against her mouth before he pulled back.

Disappointment flooded her system as she dropped her legs from around him. Moving to stand next to him, she slid an arm around his waist. Sex would apparently have to wait.

She turned to see two vehicles arriving. Mercer pulled up in his truck with Mary Grace in the passenger seat waving at them. The SUV that pulled up next to them revealed Gage, Savage, Brooks, and Leighton. She didn't know Leighton well but he'd welcomed her the same as all the others. With open arms.

Mary Grace jumped out, a bottle of champagne in her hand as Mercer hurried after her, telling her to slow down. Skye snorted as the small woman shooed him off and held out the bottle—which turned out to be sparkling cider, in deference to her pregnancy.

"Did we miss it?" Mary Grace asked.

"I haven't told her yet," Colt murmured.

"Told me what?" Skye demanded. Because what could be as important as an engagement?

He squeezed her shoulders and turned her toward the warehouse. "Why I bought this. I...might have commandeered some diamonds that Gianni stole."

She glanced up at him, eyebrows raised. He really was good at keeping secrets. "From where?"

Colt lifted a shoulder, giving her such a boyish grin that she found herself staring, hopelessly mesmerized by this man who'd stolen her heart. "He had a few safe houses the Feds were checking out."

"And we got to one of them first." Savage's voice was gleeful as he crossed his arms over his chest. "It was a treasure trove of gems and antiquities."

"Which just makes the fact that he wanted to steal a bioweapon even worse. He had enough money. He was just greedy." Gage shook his head, disgusted.

"So...you used the money to buy this warehouse?" she asked.

"A very small portion of it. I love working with you. With all of you. And I think we can do something real, something good. Help people."

"People?"

"Yeah. People who need help. Too poor to hire private security or too scared to leave their abuser. Or whatever. Regular civilians who need help. We could do a lot of good together. And I know 'help' covers a lot of ground. I just know I can't go back to working for the government. But I've got a hell of a lot of training and I want to open a consulting firm."

"We all do," Savage murmured, motioning to himself, Gage and Leighton.

"And *we* will be here to provide support and pizza," Mercer said, wrapping an arm around his wife's shoulders, drawing a smile from Skye. She really did love those two. "What you did, rescuing Mary Grace... You're one woman. Imagine what all of us could do together to help people."

Skye looked at the building, then at Colt. It sounded so simple, yet she knew it would be anything but that. She also knew she was up to the task. After all, how hard could it be to find people in need of help? Besides, she'd go stir-crazy if she couldn't use her skill set.

"You think it's nuts, don't you?" Colt murmured.

"No, I think it's insanely and utterly perfect. So...you're all moving back to Redemption Harbor?" she asked, looking at Gage, Savage and Leighton. That was a huge step. And a heck of a commitment to this thing.

They all nodded.

"We'll have to come up with a name for our company."

"Already on it," Gage said.

"We're not calling it Gage's Consulting." Savage's tone was exhausted, as if they'd had this conversation before.

"We'll have to take a vote."

Skye listened to them chatter as Mary Grace popped the top on the cider. She turned into Colt's arms and linked her fingers behind his neck. "This is huge."

"I know."

"What made you think to do this?"

He leaned down, nibbled on her ear for a moment. "We all need this, need to have a purpose, to give back to those who need it most. Leighton and Savage most of all."

Yeah, she'd gotten that vibe too. And even if Colt didn't see it, she thought Brooks might need a little emotional healing as well. "This won't be easy," she murmured.

"I know." He pulled back, looked into her eyes. "Nothing worth having is."

She narrowed her eyes at him. "What are you holding back?"

"I've already got a couple really good cases lined up."

She blinked. "How is that possible?"

"About a week before I left on my 'vacation,' one of my assets told me about this guy—a businessman in Georgia—using his shipping company as a cover to bring over women and children as slaves. Mostly from Asia."

She gritted her teeth. Slavery and the skin trade were alive and well, even today. "You tell Hernandez about it?"

"Yeah. He passed it off to the locals, who haven't done shit. I think the guy is protected."

Of course he was. "So...consulting?"

He lifted a shoulder. "Most likely consulting and security."

"This feels surreal, just starting a business like this." But she was beyond excited. The possibilities of all the good they could do...they were endless.

He raised an eyebrow. "You have other plans?"

"Only to marry you as soon as humanly possible. But I can help take down a slaver before that."

Grinning, he pulled her even closer, wrapping his arms around her tight. "This is going to work. I feel it."

She wasn't sure if he meant the company or them, but either way, she had no doubt that she and Colt were going to work out. Forever.

CHAPTER TWENTY-THREE

—What a wonderful world.—

Colt hadn't been kidding about getting married as soon as they could get a marriage license. Not even a week had passed since Colt had bought the warehouse with big plans for their new venture—and they'd already started the wheels turning on bringing down that bastard in Georgia who was selling people. Soon he'd be in jail. Or dead. And his organization would be shut down.

Today she wasn't going to think about that. Not when she was about to walk down the aisle and embark on the biggest adventure of her life.

"You're so beautiful." Mary Grace sniffled into her tissue as she stared at Skye.

Skye shifted in her kitten heels and glanced down at her cobalt blue dress. She'd opted not to do the traditional white dress and had been contemplating no dress at all, but Mary Grace had convinced her otherwise. She'd threatened that Mercer would stop providing pizza to everyone if Skye didn't wear a dress. Which was a little ridiculous, but a small price to pay. And okay, she couldn't wait to see Colt's face when she walked down the aisle.

"I do look pretty awesome," she agreed, earning a laugh from the other woman.

"I'm sorry your friend couldn't come," Mary Grace said, tucking the tissue into her small bouquet of calla lilies.

"It was last minute and I knew she probably couldn't." Skye could count on one hand the girlfriends she had, and have fingers left over. There was only one real friend from college she'd wanted to be here, but it wasn't to be. "Olivia promised to come visit in a month though, so you'll get to meet her and her daughter."

"Good. Do you need anything?"

Skye shook her head and glanced at the grandfather clock in the corner of the small guest room. "Just to get married."

"Good answer. Sit tight. I'm going to go get Colt's dad."

Skye wasn't nervous about saying her vows, but butterflies danced in her belly all the same as she perched on the little settee next to the window. Glancing out the window, she saw Colt in his tuxedo, looking sexy as always as he stood talking to Savage and Brooks. They'd set up an arbor and seating area next to the pool—which was filled with floating flowers and candles. It wasn't dark yet so they wouldn't be lit for a few hours yet. But they'd strung pretty little lights over the pool, the arbor, and all around the patio of Brooks's estate. Though patio seemed like the wrong word for such an expansive area.

It was a small wedding, with about fifty people, mostly men and women they'd worked with over the years. People they actually liked. And of course some of the people Colt had known in Redemption Harbor growing up.

When the door opened, she stood and smiled at Senior.

"You're a beautiful bride," he said, seeming only a little uncomfortable. She knew it had nothing to do with her though, and everything to do with his strained relationship with his son.

"Thank you. You clean up pretty good yourself."

He gave her a wry smile. "Thanks. Can't wait to get out of this monkey suit."

She laughed lightly and covered the distance to him, linking her arm through his. "I'm ready to do this."

"Good. I know my son is ready to marry you." His voice was full of pride as they stepped out into the hallway.

She was more than ready to marry Colt. So much that absolutely nothing would stand in her way. They'd come too far.

As she and Senior reached the French doors where she would make her "grand entrance," according to Mary Grace, she took a deep breath. This was it.

"Thank you for asking me to walk you down the aisle," Senior said quietly, his voice thick with emotion.

She swallowed hard but didn't look at him. She was afraid if she did, she might actually cry. She'd never been the type of little girl to envision her dream wedding or future husband or any of that. But when Colt had told her he wanted an actual wedding, not a courthouse one like she'd assumed, she'd been sad her parents couldn't be here. No matter what, she knew they'd have wanted to see this day. And they would have loved Colt. "Thank you for saying yes."

He cleared his throat. "I...wasn't the best father to Colt."

"You're not dead yet. There's still time to get things right."

"Yeah, I guess there is."

The French doors opened and the instrumental version of "Somewhere Over the Rainbow" started playing. She didn't need the lyrics. She knew every single word and this was the one and only request she'd had for their wedding. That this was their processional music.

As she stepped out onto the pale blue carpet runner covered with white flower petals, all she saw was Colt. Everything and everyone faded away as she walked down the makeshift aisle toward the man she loved. She'd never even thought to dream of someone so wonderful because she couldn't have imagined someone like him existed.

It seemed only seconds passed before she was standing in front of Colt. His broad shoulders stretched against the jacket of his tux and his green gaze was pinned to hers, focused and loving. She wanted to kiss him, to wrap around him and never let go. Instead she reached for his hands, taking them in hers. Touching him always grounded her.

"You're the most beautiful thing I've ever seen." His voice was low, reverent.

Throat thick, she smiled at him. "So are you."

The grin he gave her was wicked and she felt it all the way to her core. "You ready to make me an honest man?"

Laughing lightly, she turned with him toward Gage, who was their officiant—thanks to the internet. But she kept her hands firmly intertwined with Colt's. It was hard to believe she'd been afraid to tell him she loved him at one point.

Now all she wanted to do was say it every day. And she planned to, for the rest of their lives.

Seven months later

Colt stepped into the conference room of Redemption Harbor Consulting to find Skye and Savage engaged in a serious game of darts to decide who had to file the most recent paperwork.

"Your arm action is as weak as your trash talk." Skye threw a red dart, hitting the target dead center. "And I just kicked your ass. Twice."

"I don't know how, but I think you're cheating." Savage tossed the rest of his darts onto the polished table they normally used for meetings. Then he grinned when he saw Colt. "Your wife's cold, man. That's the third time I'm filing this week."

Colt would never tire of hearing her referred to as his wife. "Well I think I've got good news for both of you. For all of us. Might have a new admin assistant."

"Thank God," Savage muttered, clapping him on the shoulder once before leaving the room.

"You found someone?" Skye started boxing up all the darts from across the table.

"Maybe." He collapsed on one of the cushy seats and let his head fall back as he watched Skye. He loved seeing her so relaxed. She'd just come off a job with Savage—in which they'd stolen sensitive material from an asshole trying to blackmail his ex-partner. The two of them worked well together, and while Colt loved working with Skye, some jobs required different types of expertise. And Skye and Savage were both damn good at getting into places they shouldn't.

Skye frowned as she put the top on the dart box. Turning to him, she put her hands on her jean-clad hips. The black T-shirt she had on molded to all her curves and all he could fantasize about was peeling it up inch by inch until she was bared to him. Some days it was hard to believe that she was his and that they'd started to build this life together. "What's up? I thought you said the job was over."

"It is. I'm good. Just tired. And they insisted on paying me." He shook his head and set the check down on the table. It wasn't much, but he hadn't had the heart to turn it down because it was a matter of pride.

A neighborhood a city over had been targeted by thugs shaking down local business owners for "protection." One of the owners had stood up to them, called the cops—and ended up in the hospital with broken ribs and a concussion for his trouble. After that no one had been willing to talk. So Colt had done his thing and now the thugs were in jail and the owners had their neighborhood back. It was small time compared to the ops he'd run in the past, but he felt damn good about helping those people. Leighton had been with him for the majority of the job, but things had taken a couple weeks and he needed some rest.

Well, rest and time with Skye.

"I hope you're not too tired for naked time," she murmured, coming around the table. Straddling him, she leaned down to kiss him, rubbing her breasts against his chest. Just like that he was hard.

"I'm never too tired for that," he murmured, setting his hands on her hips. He'd missed her like crazy. They'd talked on the phone multiple times a day—and had a few rounds of phone sex—but holding her like this was a hell of a lot better.

"Get a room, you two." Gage stepped into the conference room, a slice of Mercer's pizza in his hand. Of course Mercer hadn't made it since he was home with the new baby and Mary Grace, but it was from one of his restaurants. "Preferably not one in the building."

"You better have a damn good reason for interrupting," Colt growled.

"Skye, your friend is here to see you. Olivia, the one who visited a while back. She's got her kid with her...and a duffel bag. She's moving stiffly, as if she's hurt. She's also wearing sunglasses. Inside."

Colt started to stand even as Skye slid off him. They were both quiet as they stepped out into the hallway, Gage right with them.

They'd helped two women escape their abusers since starting the company, but he hadn't thought Olivia was with anyone—not since leaving her husband years ago. No matter what her problem was, they were going to help.

When they reached the end of the hallway, stepping out into the lobby, his jaw tightened as he saw Olivia standing there looking fragile and afraid. Even if he couldn't see her eyes because of the sunglasses, her body language said it all.

Her little girl, with long black hair pulled back into a ponytail, smiled nervously when she saw him, but then pure relief crossed her expression when her gaze landed on Skye.

His wife dropped his hand and moved toward the two females faster than he'd thought possible, her legs eating up the distance in seconds.

"What happened?" Skye demanded even as six-year-old Valencia jumped into her arms. Skye might claim to be afraid of kids, but Valencia had stolen her heart—and he'd seen her cuddling Mary Grace and Mercer's new baby on more than one occasion.

The little girl was deaf, but had cochlear implants so she could hear if she chose to. Before Olivia could answer Valencia signed to Skye—who understood perfectly. Colt was still learning sign language so he was rusty but he was pretty sure she'd just said "a bad man hurt Mommy."

"Can we talk about this in private? I was hoping maybe..." Olivia's voice cracked once before she cleared her throat. "Maybe Colt could watch Valencia so we could have a few minutes to talk, just the two of us?" she asked, signing and speaking at the same time.

Skye nodded then signed to Valencia, asking her if she minded hanging out with Uncle Colt.

Valencia shook her head then wiggled in Skye's arms before cautiously stepping over to him. She'd been so relaxed the last time they visited, giggling and wanting to play video games, so whatever had happened, he had a feeling she'd seen something. Maybe even her mother hurt.

Which brought out all his rage, but he locked it down. He didn't want the little girl to sense it. When he looked at Skye, it was clear she felt the same. Her blue eyes sparked with anger as she turned to Olivia and wrapped an arm around her shoulders.

Whoever had hurt Skye's friend had made the biggest mistake of their life. Now that Olivia and Valencia had Skye and the whole crew to back her up, they were safe. And someone was going to pay.

—The End—

Thank you for reading Resurrection, the first book in my all new Redemption Harbor series. If you don't want to miss any future releases, please feel free to join my newsletter. Find the signup link on my website: http://www.katie-reus.com

ACKNOWLEDGMENTS

It's time to thank my usual crew! As always, I owe a big thanks to Kari Walker for everything you do. Joan Swan & Julie Kenner, thank you for a fun plotting week and all your help with outlining this new book and series. For Sarah, thank you for all your behind-the-scenes work that helps keep me balanced. Jaycee, thank you for another great cover. Julia, I'm grateful for your editing expertise. A big thanks to Joanna Moreno and Grace Sandvigen for helping with translations. I'm also grateful to my very understanding family. And, last but not least, thank you to God.

Red Stone Security Series
No One to Trust
Danger Next Door
Fatal Deception
Miami, Mistletoe & Murder
His to Protect
Breaking Her Rules
Protecting His Witness
Sinful Seduction
Under His Protection
Deadly Fallout
Sworn to Protect
Secret Obsession
Love Thy Enemy
Dangerous Protector
Lethal Game

Deadly Ops Series
Targeted
Bound to Danger
Chasing Danger (novella)
Shattered Duty
Edge of Danger
A Covert Affair

Redemption Harbor Series
Resurrection

The Serafina: Sin City Series
First Surrender
Sensual Surrender
Sweetest Surrender
Dangerous Surrender

O'Connor Family Series
Merry Christmas, Baby
Tease Me, Baby
It's Me Again, Baby
Mistletoe Me, Baby

Non-series Romantic Suspense
Running From the Past
Dangerous Secrets
Killer Secrets
Deadly Obsession
Danger in Paradise
His Secret Past
Retribution

Paranormal Romance
Destined Mate
Protector's Mate
A Jaguar's Kiss
Tempting the Jaguar
Enemy Mine
Heart of the Jaguar

Moon Shifter Series
Alpha Instinct
Lover's Instinct
Primal Possession
Mating Instinct
His Untamed Desire
Avenger's Heat
Hunter Reborn
Protective Instinct
Dark Protector
A Mate for Christmas

Darkness Series
Darkness Awakened
Taste of Darkness
Beyond the Darkness
Hunted by Darkness
Into the Darkness
Saved by Darkness

ABOUT THE AUTHOR

Katie Reus is the *New York Times* and *USA Today* bestselling author of the Red Stone Security series, the Darkness series and the Deadly Ops series. She fell in love with romance at a young age thanks to books she pilfered from her mom's stash. Years later she loves reading romance almost as much as she loves writing it.

However, she didn't always know she wanted to be a writer. After changing majors many times, she finally graduated summa cum laude with a degree in psychology. Not long after that she discovered a new love. Writing. She now spends her days writing dark paranormal romance and sexy romantic suspense.

For more information on Katie please visit her website: www.katiereus.com. Also find her on twitter @katiereus or visit her on facebook at: www.facebook.com/katiereusauthor.

45621516R00150

Made in the USA
Middletown, DE
09 July 2017